# SERVING UP OFF-LIMITS LOVE

JENNIFER SNOW

Recycling programs for this product may not exist in your area.

ISBN-13: 978-1-335-47086-7

Serving Up Off-Limits Love



For questions and comments about the quality of this book, please contact us at CustomerService@Harlequin.com.

Harlequin Enterprises ULC
22 Adelaide St. West, 41st Floor
Toronto, Ontario M5H 4E3, Canada
www.Harlequin.com

HarperCollins Publishers
Macken House, 39/40 Mayor Street Upper,
Dublin 1, D01 C9W8, Ireland
www.HarperCollins.com

**Printed in U.S.A.**

1 2 3 4 5 6 7 8 9 10 HDC 28 27 26 25

*An enchanting new Harlequin Romance trilogy from USA TODAY bestselling author Jennifer Snow.*

**From Amalfi with Amore**

*Postcards from Italy...*

Three years ago, billionaire brothers Domenico, Leo and Mario opened the Kasa Island Resort, a small slice of heaven just off the Amalfi Coast. Surrounded by beautiful scenery, luxurious accommodations and fascinating guests, the brothers are determined to honor their father's legacy by preserving this perfect island escape...

But there's trouble in paradise when each of the Kasa brothers meets his match...and has his life turned upside down. Friendship, family ties and the future of the resort—all of these are threatened when the spark of attraction flares into an inferno.

Will the Kasa brothers risk playing with fire to follow their hearts?

Find out in...

Domenico and Adriana's story...
*Serving Up Off-Limits Love*
Available now!

And look out for Leo's and Mario's stories,
Both coming soon!

Dear Reader,

I love to travel and Europe has always been a favorite destination of mine—the cultures, the scenery, the food and wine...but most of all the resorts! In writing the Kasa Island series, I wanted to create a luxury resort setting that readers would dream of visiting, and having it owned by three billionaire brothers made it that much more exotic.

Enemies to lovers has always been a favorite trope of mine to read and write, so this love story between Adriana and Domenico was a fun one! The tension, the heat and the chemistry between these two are undeniable, and the added element of a forbidden romance makes it that much more exciting!

I hope you enjoy your experience on Kasa Island!

XO

*Jen*

**Jennifer Snow** is a *USA TODAY* bestselling author and screenwriter of over forty novels and thirty screenplays. She writes romantic comedies and thrillers for Harlequin, Grand Central, Entangled, Penguin Random House and Thomas & Mercer, and her books have won awards such as the Booksellers' Best Award and have been translated into many foreign languages, as well as optioned for film. Her produced credits include *14 Love Letters* (Hallmark), *Christmas Lucky Charm* (UPtv) and *Mistletoe & Molly* (UPtv), and she had eight TV MOWs airing on various networks in 2023, including *Christmas in Maple Hills*, *Sworn Justice* and *Christmas at the Amish Bakery*. More information can be found on her website at jennifersnowauthor.com.

*Serving Up Off-Limits Love*
is Jennifer Snow's debut title for Harlequin Romance.

Visit the Author Profile page at Harlequin.com
for more titles from Jennifer Snow.

To Reagan—
I'll always cherish the memories of our travel adventures.

# CHAPTER ONE

DOMENICO KASA HAD drawn the shortest straw and was now ducking for his life.

The stainless-steel spatula whipped past his right ear and landed with a deafening clatter on the tiled kitchen floor. While the utensil would have dented Domenico's forehead if he hadn't reacted so quickly, the knife in the chef's other hand was more concerning.

But the recently *fired* head chef of the Kasa de Paradise Resort wasn't crazy enough to throw that. Was he?

"Christian, settle down." Domenico selected the biggest, heaviest frying pan hanging above the center island in the pristine thousand-square-foot kitchen. Holding it as a shield, he moved closer to the door. "We both knew this was coming."

A string of curse words muttered in French was the only response as the chef resumed slicing the onion on the cutting board in front of him. The knife moved with speed and precision.

Then the thin slices of onion sizzled as they hit the pan of melted butter on the stove.

Domenico's stomach growled and his mouth watered as the smell of caramelized onions filled the kitchen. Chef Dubois's French onion soup was the best he'd ever tasted in his twenty-seven years. If only their world-famous chef wasn't also a world-famous womanizer.

Firing the best cook they'd had working at the resort since they opened three years ago on the private island off the coast of Naples, Italy, went against all common sense...but several sexual harassment complaints from wealthy, married, *influential* guests within a few days made this decision an easy one.

"The women here are not like the women in my country," Chef Dubois said, the knife swinging.

Domenico was fairly certain women didn't appreciate being groped in *any* country, but he remained silent until everything sharp was out of Christian's reach. "Regardless, we're letting you go."

"We?"

Right. *He*. He was letting the chef go. His older brothers were hiding under their respective beds. "We will obviously pay your travel costs back to Paris and a month's severance, which should help until you find another job."

Christian laughed. "I turned down four offers d'emploi to come here to this…this…this…" He gestured wildly with the knife, his look of disgust not exactly the expression most people wore when they spoke about Kasa de Paradise.

The luxury resort located on the island owned by the Kasa brothers consisted of twenty-five private villas, various dining options from a formal restaurant to a beachside barbecue, two spa and fitness facilities with tennis courts and golf courses, an infinity pool overlooking the sea, and acres of lush flora and fauna. Daily excursions—relaxing boat rides to zip-lining for the more adventurous traveler—took guests to the remote areas of the island to explore the unspoiled landscape. Nothing was off-limits or unattainable.

With guests transported by boat from Naples to the island, the resort was reserved by the week. Only the most elite could afford the thirty-thousand-euro price tag for the all-inclusive vacation experience.

Movie stars, musicians, politicians and high-end executives were the clientele at Kasa de Paradise, and not one in three years had ever worn the *who farted?* expression the chef wore right now.

"Then you won't have any trouble landing on

your feet," Domenico said while the man continued to search for the right insult.

Christian stared at him. "You want to fire me two days before the reviewer from *Travel Island* magazine arrives?"

Not particularly, but the chef had left them little choice. Among a million other ethical reasons, if Linda Frank, the American reviewer for the influential international travel publication, heard about the chef's inappropriate behavior with the guests, they could kiss their hopes for a flattering review goodbye. Unfortunately, they might have to anyway. Nightly four-course meals, tasting menus and event catering weren't going to be easy to execute without a head chef.

"We hope to have a replacement by then," Domenico said.

"In two days? Ha!" More chopping, more muttering, more cussing.

Time to grow a set of balls the size of coconuts. "Christian, I need you to pack your things immediately. We have a boat waiting to take you back to the mainland."

The chef stopped and dropped the knife, glancing at him as though only now realizing he was serious. "You're firing *moi*?"

*For the last twenty minutes now.*

The anarchy that followed resulted in a bandaged hand for Domenico and resort security—all four of the two-hundred-fifty-pound ex-military—"escorting" Christian Dubois to his living quarters and then to the boat waiting to take him back to Naples.

"Damn," Domenico muttered, joining his brothers where the other two *uninjured* Kasas had been watching the fiasco on the dock from the safety and comfort of the resort's main office. "That went well," he said, collapsing into a plush leather chair near the floor-to-ceiling window overlooking the property. Sixty-five acres that they'd purchased when they'd sold their family's hotel chain, after their father's death. The resort they'd designed, built, and turned into one of the hottest high-end destinations in the Mediterranean in less than four years would have made their father proud. Leonardo Kasa Sr. had always said he was building the hotel chain for their future, but when the man had gotten sick, he'd told the boys to sell the properties and use the money to do whatever made them happy.

Failing their father's legacy with an unsuccessful venture wasn't an option.

"At least it wasn't your tennis hand," his oldest brother, Leo, said, nodding to the bandage the resort's medic had wrapped around Domenico's left hand.

Thank God the chef's aim wasn't as fantastic

as his French onion soup. Otherwise Domenico might have required stitches.

"Yeah, don't you have an evening lesson scheduled with Mrs. Conway?" his other brother, Mario, asked. The deep grin spreading across his face told Domenico that he did *now*.

"When do the Conways check out? Tell me it's tomorrow." Guests ran from Sunday to Saturday, and the Conways—two real estate tycoons, a husband-and-wife team—had originally booked one week…which they kept extending. Due to a lull in reservations during the fall months, the brothers weren't turning away their money.

A former professional tennis player, Domenico offered lessons as an added benefit to the resort, and Mrs. Conway was booking every available time slot in his schedule…but somehow her skills continued to get worse.

"They rebooked for another week," Leo said, checking the reservation files on his desk.

Fantastic. While Linda Frank was there, Domenico would have additional stress he did not need. "You have to start telling them we're full," he said. Mrs. Conway, a five-foot-ten forty-five-year-old redhead with surgically enhanced…everything…might not have appreciated Chef Dubois's advances, but she seemed to be encouraging any attention Domenico was willing to bestow.

"We're *not* full," Leo said.

Domenico turned to look at Mario, who was reviewing the new resort brochures. "Why not?" When they'd first opened the resort, they were full all the time. Lately reservations had been down at least thirty percent. They'd expected a dip after the initial opening, but thirty percent would put them in operational danger zone if it continued.

"Hey, I just got back from Spain, remember?" Mario was immediately on the defensive. "Sourcing that expensive wine the reviewer raved about last month in her article about Spanish vineyards."

Mario was in charge of marketing and promotions of the resort, but he was off on sourcing expeditions more than he was on the island. And Spain seemed to be a favorite port of call. Domenico couldn't help but wonder if something other than vineyards was occupying his brother's time on these trips. The expense reports seemed to suggest so.

"Besides, I keep telling you both that we need to offer open reservations during the slower months. You two refuse to listen."

"Exclusivity is what Kasa Island is about. Guests book a full week or nothing." Limiting reservations to clientele who could afford the cost of a full week's stay gave the resort their high-end, luxury status. Allowing guests to check in for a few nights increased costs and lowered the public perception of the resort. "I'm with Dom on this one," Leo said to Mario. "You need to find other ways to bring in guests."

"Hey, who convinced Travel Island to come here?" Mario said, setting the brochures on the desk and stretching his long legs out in front of him.

"You can't ride that stroke of good fortune forever," Leo said.

"I can and I will," Mario retorted.

"Speaking of…handsy chef did point out *one* minor issue. Who is going to look after the kitchen?" Domenico asked. He hoped his brothers had been working out a new plan while he was being attacked.

The sous-chef was fantastic and they could certainly help in the interim, but the reviewer wouldn't be impressed. They'd have to go through their stack of applicants to see if there was anyone qualified who hadn't yet accepted another position and could be there on a moment's notice… They had no time to put out a job posting and conduct interviews. But getting someone to accept a position at Kasa Island shouldn't be difficult. They paid a generous salary, and the living quarters for the staff were located in a private, secluded section of the island, near the beach. The sound of the waves at night crashing along the shore was Domenico's favorite part of island living.

Mario and Leo exchanged looks. "We have someone."

Oh no.

Fine hairs on Domenico's arms stood up, and his gut tightened. "Don't say it."

"I had to, man," Leo said with a shrug. "Adriana is the only person I trust, and she agreed to help us out to get us through the reviewer's stay."

Adriana Bellarini. His brother's ex-girlfriend.

The Bellarini family had been long-time friends with the Kasas. The brothers had grown up with Adriana and her brother, Alex, which played a huge part in why Leo insisted on remaining friends with Adriana, despite the fact she'd broken his heart.

How much of this decision was based on needing a chef, and how much was Leo's own desire to have Adriana on the island? Domenico knew his brother had offered her the executive chef position numerous times. Luckily she kept turning him down. "Doesn't she have her own restaurant to take care of?"

"She's willing to do us this favor. Alex is looking after the kitchen at Bellarini's for a week," Leo said, with a look that suggested Domenico should be relieved.

He wasn't. And it annoyed him that his brothers had made this executive decision without him. He and Adriana had once been the best of friends, until his tennis training had taken him all over the world. In his absence, she'd fallen for his older brother.

"I suppose she's on her way?"

Leo nodded. "Arriving later today. And you'll have to meet her at the dock and get her settled—I have a Zoom call with potential guests."

Domenico's jaw clenched as he stood. "And I can't change your mind?" He already knew the answer.

"Sorry. We need her," Leo said.

He glanced at Mario, but this time it was the older Kasa brothers who were sticking together.

"Fine," Domenico said, walking toward the office door. "I'll be overseeing every move she makes, but if—*when*—things go sideways, remember I had nothing to do with this decision."

There was no one else Adriana would abandon her family restaurant for. But when Leo Kasa needed her, she was there, especially when a reviewer from *Travel Island* magazine would be at Kasa de Paradise that week. A fantastic review from Linda Frank would do wonders for the resort, but also, her own struggling restaurant could use the boost from the praise of an influential reviewer.

Linda was in high demand, and her reviews were coveted. She was selective about the resorts she chose to visit, and her opinion was gospel all over the world. A rave review from Linda could have a resort at full capacity within the week. A bad review…

Well, she wouldn't entertain that possibility.

This possible added benefit that could come from helping Leo only increased her anxiety as she boarded the *Passage to Paradise* that evening.

"Miss Bellarini, welcome aboard," said the shuttle boat captain, Jon, extending a hand and taking her small suitcase as he helped her aboard. He was a short, stocky man with marine-themed tattoos—a former captain of a cruise ship who'd opted for the peace and serenity of small excursions working for the Kasa brothers.

"Thank you," she said, taking a seat along the bench at the front, looking out toward the sea. Kasa de Paradise wasn't visible from the mainland, but once they cleared the narrows in the harbor, the resort would come into view.

She'd been on the private island a few times to help Leo design the magnificent kitchen, but then she'd handed the golden oven mitts to the first of six different chefs in four years. He'd offered her the position, but she'd easily turned it down. As beautiful as Kasa Island was, her heart was in her family restaurant. She was desperate to prove to herself that her late father hadn't made the wrong decision leaving it in her hands and not her brother's. Which meant full-time commitment and dedication.

She also feared Leo's offer came from a secret hope that the two of them might rekindle the flame they'd once had. Adriana refused to give him that unfair hope. They were great friends, despite their breakup, and she cherished that enough not to ruin things with another attempt at a relationship when she didn't feel the right spark for Leo anymore.

They'd grown up together. Their love was young love fueled heavily by their family's desire to see a Bellarini-Kasa union—an official combining of their families. At one time, Adriana had thought maybe that union would have occurred with a different Kasa brother, but once Domenico started his tennis career, he'd never looked back. He'd seemed to forget all about her, as evidenced by the photos of him dating other female competitors in the tabloids, which had hurt. Leo had been there, feeling a similar disappointment that his brother seemed laser-focused on just one thing—tennis—and not the family or the family business anymore. The two had bonded over it, and later, fear of disappointing their families had kept her from ending things sooner.

Luckily their friendship and childhood bond had helped ease the heartache of a breakup enough to stay great friends.

Domenico's betrayal had caused a different kind of heartache, one that hadn't completely eased.

The boat pulled away from the dock, and she bit her lip. "How's the water?" Choppy waves reflected the low setting sun, and the mild ocean breeze blew her long, dark hair away from her face as she surveyed them with a nervous look.

"Smooth sailing," the captain said. "The *Passage to Paradise* was designed to glide over the roughest waves. You won't feel but a slight sway, Miss Bellarini."

Everything on Kasa de Paradise was designed with executive-level guests' comfort in mind. Suddenly Adriana was nervous about more than the waves. The resort boasted the best of everything—accommodations, amenities, entertainment and…food.

Would Leo have immediately thought of her if he knew Bellarini's wasn't doing so great?

Maybe that was why he had. She'd never told him that the restaurant was struggling. She knew he must have suspected it when the place was practically empty whenever he stopped by for dinner on the mainland. He believed in her and her talent, and she valued his friendship and support.

Her brother, Alex, on the other hand, thought Bellarini's menu was the problem. He claimed that the decades-old patron favorites needed to be replaced with fresh new dishes, including some healthier choices. Over the last year and a half, they'd head-butted on the issue over and over.

While she knew Alex was right…to some degree…she refused to change Bellarini's into something it wasn't. Food from the Campania region was all about familiar family recipes passed along from generation to generation. People ate there when they wanted an authentically prepared Italian meal. Her parents had ultimately trusted her with the restaurant. She was determined to make Bellarini's successful again without sacrificing what made it a cherished family destination in the beginning.

She cleared her throat. "So, what happened to Chef Dubois?" she asked Jon.

"Complaints from guests."

Chef Dubois was one of the top chefs in Paris. He'd worked at Michelin-starred restaurants and had secured world acclaim as an inventor of flavor. If his cooking didn't measure up… Her stomach knotted.

"Complaints? About his food?"

"About his wandering hands," Jon said, turning to her with a smile.

She relaxed and laughed. "Well, they don't have to worry about that with me."

Running the restaurant and working long hours doing meal prep, ordering supplies, trying the new recipes Alex insisted she at least consider, Adriana hadn't been on a real date in… three years? She wouldn't even try to remember the last time she'd had sex. At twenty-six, she was practically a virgin again.

Three years single? Could it really be that long?

"The Kasa brothers are very excited that you agreed to come," the captain said.

She knew Leo was pleased, and Mario wouldn't care either way, but she had her doubts that Domenico had readily agreed to this week-long situation. Since they'd drifted apart years before, he barely acknowledged her presence when they were forced to share the same air, and she'd never fully understood what had happened to make him dislike her. He'd been the one to forget about her and their connection while he was off chasing his dream—and gorgeous athletes.

But she had no time to think about that this week. She needed to secure a great review for the resort and her skills in the kitchen.

To help her own struggling restaurant.

"Are Domenico and Mario on the island?" Maybe they were away and she'd only have to deal with Leo.

"Mr. Mario is leaving for Greece tonight, but Mr. Domenico never leaves the island. I can't remember the last time he stepped onto the *Passage to Paradise*."

Right.

Lush greenery bordered by acres of soft golden sand was a welcoming sight moments later as Kasa Island graced the horizon. She could see the resort's main building standing high on the tallest peak of the island, its rustic stone structure and terra-cotta rooftop echoing the style of an Apulian trullo—prioritizing a simplicity that complemented the natural surroundings. Its large courtyard extending along the back provided space for relaxation and tranquility. Even the white-capped waves crashing against the shore below looked peaceful. As Adriana breathed in the sweet, salty air, she felt some of the tension release from her shoulders.

If she had to be away from her restaurant, there was nowhere more appealing.

Kasa Island catered to all kinds of wealthy

clientele, but they seemed to have one thing in common—a desire for peace and calmness they sometimes didn't even realize they needed.

Shading her eyes from the setting sun, she saw Domenico on the dock.

He was gorgeous. Tall, dark and traditionally handsome, but he always wore a scowl—at least when he saw her.

The exact one he was wearing now, she observed as the boat drew closer.

She'd been right about one thing—Domenico Kasa wasn't thrilled that she was there to save the day.

No pressure at all.

If he told her where one more thing was in this kitchen, she'd lose it.

"Over here are the..."

"Domenico! Stop, please." Adriana struggled to keep her tone calm and polite. Damn Leo for handing her off to Domenico, but he'd had Zoom calls with potential guests. Now she found herself alone with the brother she'd been hoping to avoid. She and Domenico had once been the closest of friends among the Kasa and Bellarini kids...when they were like, ten, before his ego developed and his face was splashed all over the tabloids. *The playboy of tennis* was her "favorite" of all the taglines.

Domenico turned toward her. She took a steadying breath before saying, “I’m sure you have a million things to do other than show me around, and I *did* design this kitchen, remember?”

She saw his jaw clench as he nodded. His face had yet to display anything other than irritation, and his welcoming grunt on the dock had made it clear having her there was not his idea.

Why was *he* so annoyed?

*She* was the one leaving her family restaurant in the hands of her brother, who might turn the place completely vegan by the time she got back. “Is there a problem, Domenico?” They could be adults about whatever was bothering him.

Not that she cared, but things would be less stressful that week if he wasn’t scowling like a petulant child whenever she had the misfortune of seeing him.

“I don’t think you’re qualified to run the kitchen.”

The bluntness of the words was a little shocking. She hadn’t thought he’d actually come out with the truth. And the gut-punch effect had everything to do with the fact that the same words had come from her father on his deathbed. The man had been suffering from dementia, and she had desperately chosen to believe he hadn’t meant them.

Domenico Kasa, however, a hundred percent did. Good thing his opinion of her was something she hadn't cared about in a long time.

"Well, lucky for you, you're wrong. So if you could get out, I can start making you eat your words." Which was all he'd be eating if she had her way. That mouth didn't deserve to enjoy anything she made. Her eyes dropped to said mouth, and her own went slightly dry. Unlike Leo's thin lips, Domenico's were full, soft-looking… Tom Hardy lips…

In fact, the brothers didn't share any common traits. Whereas Leo was just over five-foot-eleven, Domenico towered over her at six-foot-three. Leo was athletic but slim compared to Domenico's wider frame. While both brothers had brown hair and blue eyes, Domenico's short, messy waves were darker, and the blue of his eyes matched the color of the Mediterranean Sea.

A mesmerizing sea a woman could get lost in…and ultimately get seasick. She was sure his string of flings over the years could attest to that.

He coughed, covering his mouth, and her gaze flew back to his. "This review is important."

*That* they could agree on.

She needed a good review as well, not that she was sharing that information with him. As soon as he left, she was getting to work on the menu.

Dinner service had been taken care of by the sous-chef and the rest of the kitchen staff. Now the kitchen was all hers for the evening. "I'm going to familiarize myself with the menu right away…as soon as you leave," she said.

Hint hint.

"Just so we're clear, I'm going to be around… a lot."

"Fantastic. But just so we're clear, you need to stay out of my way so I can do my job. As you said, this review is important."

Domenico nodded, folding his arms across his chest.

Seeing the bandages wrapped around his hand, she asked, "What happened?"

"Chef Dubois."

The laugh that escaped her was louder than she'd intended.

Domenico raised his left eyebrow. "You think it's funny?"

Adriana shook her head, composing herself. Barely. "No… I just think there are circumstances where I'd be tempted to stab you myself."

He opened his mouth to say something, then paused and shook his head. "Nope. I'm not doing this with you."

"Doing what?"

"This verbal sparring you somehow drag me into."

"*I* drag *you*…"

"I'm late for a tennis lesson," he said, checking his watch.

One he didn't sound thrilled about. "People still want you to teach them?"

His eyes narrowed slightly as he paused near the kitchen door.

Why had she egged him on? She should have let him leave.

"I once competed internationally."

"Once." What was wrong with her? Irritating him was far too much fun. She didn't know why, but she enjoyed watching his cool, calm demeanor unravel, giving her a glimpse at a different guy underneath. A slightly frazzled, easily ruffled guy. One who wasn't always so in control of his emotions. A glimpse of the sweet, insecure boy she once knew.

She envisioned steam escaping through his ears as he said, "If you don't need anything else…"

"I didn't need anything in the first place," she said, returning her attention to the menu.

"I meant what I said. Expect to be seeing a lot of me in here," he said, storming out of the kitchen.

Alone, Adriana breathed a sigh of relief. Then,

as she scanned the kitchen, a slight apprehension filled her chest.

Was Domenico right to be questioning her abilities to pull this off? She'd certainly had her doubts in the last eight hours…

No. She would not let him do that to her. Who was he to question her skills? She was at least still pursuing a career she loved. He'd walked away from his.

Adriana sighed, the rationale not doing much to calm her mind.

This week would be challenging, and it had very little to do with the menu.

# CHAPTER TWO

HE SHOULD HAVE put up more of a fight with his brothers. Adriana being here wasn't a good idea. She might be a great Italian chef, but the resort needed someone more well-rounded…

An image of her curvy figure, hugged by her chef jacket, which did absolutely nothing to downplay her appeal, flashed in his mind.

More well-rounded with their *culinary skills…* less so everywhere else.

He ran a hand over his hair as he headed toward the tennis courts. His lack of confidence in her abilities wasn't the only thing weighing heavy on him.

The Kasa kids and the Bellarini kids had grown up together, their families generational friends. His father had grown up with Alberto Bellarini, too. And out of all the kids, he and Adriana had been the closest. Inseparable every summer, actually—up until he started going away to tennis training camps every available moment of his young life. They'd drifted apart then…and somehow over one of those teenage summers, she'd drifted straight into Leo's arms. Family events had definitely been different seeing her with his brother. Not that he cared or was jealous or anything—it was just…weird. She'd been his friend first for all those years.

Did she even remember that? She didn't seem to. Not a "hey, remember when we…" or "wanna hang out like old times?" Nope. She'd been completely wrapped up in Leo all of a sudden and barely acknowledged his existence. Which was totally fine.

But how could she have forgotten the letters? They'd written actual letters to one another whenever he was away—deep, vulnerable, emotion-filled, sometimes funny letters. Hundreds of them over the years, and they'd shared dreams, secrets, doubts… He'd thought they were connecting—falling in love—through those letters.

He still had every single one of them.

How could they not have meant anything to her?

Clearly his ability to read signals was completely off. Perhaps that was why every relationship he'd ever had was surface-level and short-lived.

Adriana's betrayal had really messed him up in the romance department.

He hadn't seen her since she'd ended things

romantically with Leo, and he'd been okay with that. They'd both grown into different people over the years.

Her loud, overly expressive personality and sharp tongue were not his style. Her open, transparent nature only made him more suspicious of her intentions with his brother. No one was *that* genuinely sincere and easygoing. He liked the women he dated to be more reserved, more polished and serious…more like him.

And absolutely the opposite of the woman wearing a tennis outfit that barely covered her body, waving to him now as he approached the floodlit Astroturf courts.

"Hey you, I was starting to think I'd been stood up," Pricilla Conway said, a playful pout on her lips, but a scolding look in her eyes that suggested he'd better not be late again.

Reminding her that he owned the resort and wasn't a hired tennis instructor would be rude, so he smiled politely. Making each guest feel treasured was the aim of Kasa de Paradise. No matter how irritating the guest.

"Sorry… I was introducing our *temporary* chef to the kitchen."

This week couldn't go by fast enough. The reviewer's visit was stressing him out. She was evaluating everything—not just the food. In the last few days, he'd barely slept, taking on extra responsibility to make sure the resort was at its finest—checking all the guest room amenities and ensuring the air-conditioning was working as they'd gotten a heads-up from another resort that Linda often insisted on changing rooms multiple times during her stay. He'd personally replaced all the lights along the resort trails as they'd heard she enjoyed late-night strolls. He'd even re-tested all the emergency evacuation equipment and ensured *Passage to Paradise* met all operation codes and standards, even though Jon was always on top of that. There wasn't a thing out of place, and all staff knew to expect to be on their A game—more than ever.

The Kasa brothers needed a sparkling review.

"Yes, I noticed Chef Dubois leaving on the boat this afternoon. I apologize for causing a stir."

He doubted there was a day that went by that Mrs. Conway *didn't* cause a stir. He unzipped a tennis racket and handed it to her. The woman wore a different tight and revealing tennis outfit each time she played, yet she didn't own a racket.

Or seem to get any better at using one.

"No, you were right to file your complaint. We hope Chef Dubois's actions didn't negatively impact your stay too much."

She waved a hand. "I'm used to the attention, darling. You like my hair?" she asked, tossing her red curls. "Talia at the salon is a miracle worker. I've threatened to take her with me when we leave."

It looked the same as it did every day. Blazing, fiery red—a warning light she was attempting to use as a beacon.

"It looks great," he said, thinking about the way Adriana's dark hair had shone in the light as she'd stepped off the *Passage de Paradise* earlier that evening. Her natural copper highlights had reflected the sun's warmth.

"You seem distracted tonight," Pricilla said, touching his shoulder. He tensed as she moved closer, her breasts against his chest, the view of the ample cleavage distracting. And not in a good way. She was far too forward and obvious in her interest to appeal to him in the slightest, and she was a married woman. Not to mention a very vocal guest that liked getting her way.

So far, he'd mastered the art of turning down her not-so-subtle advances without damaging her ego. Leo and Mario had both reassured him that he didn't need to teach the woman if he was uncomfortable, but he wasn't intimidated by her—annoyed mostly.

"Just an eventful day," he said with a forced breezy air despite the tightening anxiety in his chest.

"Yes, you are under a lot of pressure," she

said in a babying tone that sounded like she was speaking to a three-year-old. "Why don't we cancel the lesson for tonight."

Best idea he'd heard all day.

"And head down to the beach..." Her breath was close to his ear, and her voice was more like a purr.

He forced a breath, removing her hands from his shoulders. "Nope," he said with a forced laugh. "I promised you we'd improve your game so you can show off at the country club back in California...next week," he added for good measure. He really hoped she would be leaving next week. How much more of her inappropriate advances could he take without snapping? "So, let's get to work." He stepped away to unzip his own racket.

"Are you sure your hand is well enough? I still can't believe you got stabbed defending my honor." The silky, smooth, flirtatious tone had the opposite of its intended effect on him.

Obviously the wedding band Mrs. Conway wore and the fact that her husband was in a chalet a block away meant nothing to her. "My hand is fine, and the resort has a one strike policy regarding complaints from guests."

How many strikes would Leo afford Adriana?

They couldn't afford even one. Linda Frank's opinion could either skyrocket the resort's success or cause it to plummet with a few typed words. Allowing the reviewer here without a permanent chef might be a mistake… Was it too late to postpone the visit?

"You're sure?" Mrs. Conway said.

"Absolutely." Man, he couldn't wait to get this lesson over with so he could take the stress of his day out on some serves from the automatic machine—the only "partner" on the island who could keep up with him.

Pricilla released an *okay, your loss* sigh as she moved to the other side of the net, her hips swaying back and forth, each step giving him the intended glimpse of her butt. "I think you just like seeing me sweat."

He was pretty sure that was *her* guilty pleasure, not his. "Alright, I'll serve first," he said, placing an extra tennis ball in his shorts pocket and tossing the other up in the air.

He swung, and as it sailed over the net, he forced his thoughts away from Adriana. Focusing his full attention on the other woman at Kasa de Paradise who made him completely uncomfortable, who he'd *also* have to put up with during one of the most stressful weeks of his life.

Adriana yawned as she reviewed Chef Dubois's menus for the week and verified that they had enough stock and produce for the variations she intended to make. It was too bad that the chef couldn't keep his hands to himself, because he was really on top of things in the kitchen.

She flipped the pages to the next morning's breakfast prep. Her eyes bulged as she flipped and flipped again. Three full pages of breakfast items?

Was it too late to sneak back onto a boat to the mainland?

The resort promised guests anything and everything they could possibly want, but fourteen variations of eggs? Whatever happened to menu rotation? Cycling the offerings? Surely this was a little overkill.

Unfortunately, *overkill* could be used to describe a lot of things on Kasa Island. Now Adriana was expected to deliver with the same attention to detail and elite-level hospitality.

It was after eleven p.m., and the prep work alone would take hours. She normally would have had the sous-chef and the team do it, but that evening after briefly meeting with the kitchen staff, she'd given them all the rest of the night off, wanting time to refamiliarize herself with the setup and get ready to take charge in the busy kitchen the next day. No wonder she'd seen a few snickers and giggles as they'd readily—and quickly—escaped the kitchen.

The resort might only have a maximum of

fifty guests at a time and fifty staff members, but a hundred people were a lot to impress.

*Linda Frank* would take a lot to impress.

Maybe Domenico was right. Maybe she wasn't the right chef to help them that week. His unconcealed disdain had been a source of fuel for her all evening, an overwhelming desire to prove Domenico Kasa wrong. But now, exhausted and feeling the pressure mount, her confidence waned.

She sighed. Better get to prepping…

Two hours later, removing her chef's jacket, she hung it on the hook near the walk-in freezer. Feeling the late-night heat on her skin, she opened the door and stepped inside.

Immediate relief.

Releasing her hair from the messy bun at the top of her head, she took several deep breaths. Goose bumps collected on her bare arms in her tank top, but she relished the cold, knowing the moment she stepped back out, the intense heat would suffocate her again.

At Bellarini's, she kept her kitchen AC on full blast. Here it didn't seem to matter. Even the sun long ago disappearing over the sea had done nothing to cool the island. Even the slight breeze was warm and wet, coating her entire body with a light gleam of moisture.

She yawned again and blinked the exhaustion

from her eyes. Making the decision to come to the island had been easy, and she hadn't felt the burden of the responsibility until now.

She checked her watch. Almost midnight and the next day would start before five a.m. Leo had assigned her a guest suite instead of a room in the staff quarters as the resort wasn't at full capacity. She longed to crawl into the king-size four-poster bed with the heavenly soft down-filled pillows she knew were awaiting her.

She'd made a good start that evening, and she still had the following full day to finalize the new evening menu and get the kitchen staff up to speed on her changes.

Thank God Domenico had stayed away that evening. He was an annoyance she couldn't afford. And she didn't want him to see the changes to the menu.

A slight pang of guilt hit her. Taking a gamble like this—possibly at the resort's expense—was wrong, but she needed this reviewer to taste her food. The dishes Bellarini's specialized in. It was her restaurant's only hope. It had spent too many years in the red, and if they didn't start making profits again soon, she'd be forced to shut the doors.

She picked up her cell phone and opened the message thread with Alex. Her last message, Just checking in, had been read and answered.

Of course.

He hadn't even tried to conceal his excitement at having control over Bellarini's for the week.

Any torment she felt about using this opportunity to her advantage dissipated. She needed to generate new appreciation for Bellarini's. Restaurant reviewers had given up visiting a long time ago. The restaurant was no longer new and impressive. They were simply a nostalgic landmark in the small Naples neighborhood without enough regulars to keep the doors open, but still paying for the prime real estate spot along the high-traffic touristy street.

Besides, why should she feel guilty about replacing menu items with dishes she excelled at making? The Kasa brothers wanted a shining review, right?

She was rationalizing to ease the guilt, and it was working until…

The memory of Domenico's piercing, untrusting gaze made her shiver. When had he developed a stare that seemed to look straight through her as though they hadn't spent their formative years together? They'd been best friends. They'd shared everything.

Through the letters.

Letters she cherished while he was away. Letters she'd read over and over, hearing his voice in her mind as she'd read. Letters she'd written revealing all her own stories, passions, doubts… Those letters back then had been everything.

But since he'd started going to tennis camps, he always came back more distant, more reserved. The year he'd turned sixteen, the tabloids said he was rumored to be dating a tennis pro from the US. Her heart had shattered, and the letters had stopped. Her sadness and that feeling of loss had her accepting Leo's affection. When Domenico had returned that year to find her dating Leo, he'd practically turned into a stranger… Someone she didn't recognize. Someone who acted as though she didn't exist.

Well, his loss, because she was a great friend. She didn't miss him or their connection one little bit.

She took one last cooling breath. Then, opening the door, she jumped, seeing Domenico standing a foot away. Her hand flew to her accelerated heart.

Hearing the freezer door close behind him, Domenico jumped even higher as he swung around toward her. "Adriana! What were you doing in there?"

"Cooling off," she said, fighting to calm her frantic pulse. "What are you doing in *here*?"

He didn't answer.

His gaze had dropped lower, to her chest. As she glanced down, her cheeks grew hot. The cold from the fridge had turned her nipples into two hard buds poking through the fabric of her tank top.

A flicker of interest registered in Domenico's eyes, and Adriana's embarrassment quickly turned to annoyance.

Oh sure, *those* he liked.

She snapped her fingers in front of her chest, and his gaze whipped up to meet hers. "What are you doing here?" she asked again.

"I was hungry," he mumbled, turning his attention to the smaller fridge.

Adriana moved across the kitchen and shut the door. "Go to the twenty-four-hour snack shop. The kitchen's closed."

"It's my kitchen."

"The kitchen belongs to the chef, and this one is closed. Everything has already been sanitized, and it's getting late. I'm not staying to clean it up again." She didn't want him lingering. He was sure to notice the extra ingredients she'd taken out and prepared for some of her popular Italian dishes. Seeing her own recipes on the counter, she quickly closed the notebook.

"I'll clean up when I'm done," he said.

"Or you could get out. You shouldn't be eating this late anyway." She raised an eyebrow and jerked her head toward his stomach.

A perfect six-pack was visible through the

sweaty shirt clinging to his rock-hard body. Of the Kasa brothers, Domenico had the most muscular build. His broad shoulders and tapered waist gave him the illusion of being bigger than he actually was. Unfortunately, his arguable status as the hottest Kasa brother did nothing to move him to the top of the list as her favorite. Not anymore, at least. He was far too serious and arrogant and closed off. When had that transition happened?

No doubt his early success and the fact that he had women dropping at his feet had played huge roles.

And she refused to make the mistake of wondering what might happen if she pulled back those layers to uncover the guy she once knew. She had no interest in finding out what was beneath Domenico's suddenly cool exterior.

None at all.

"Are you implying that I'm fat?" he asked, eyes wide.

Adriana shrugged, loving the increasing annoyance in his tone. Why did she derive so much pleasure from irritating him? It was like a drug. Once she started, she couldn't stop herself.

Unfortunately, he accepted her teasing as a challenge. He whipped the shirt off over his head and flexed his stomach.

Keeping her mouth closed proved impossible.

The outline of the muscles beneath the fabric had lied. They weren't just perfectly sculpted with tanned obliques dipping below the waistband of his shorts. They were drool-worthy. She licked her lips as she scanned the muscular chest and shoulders, drinking in the sight of him as though he were a drop of fresh water in a salty ocean. Her pulse raced, and she prayed he couldn't hear her heart pounding or read the effect he was having on her.

He grinned. "Care to take back your insult?"

She turned away, her need for air at a pivotal point. "All I'm saying is that eventually the late-night eating will catch up to you."

"I'll take my chances," he said, reopening the fridge door. "What can I eat that won't make a mess?"

She could think of something.

Where had that thought come from?

Probably the sight of his big biceps braced against the fridge. Since when did tennis players have big, sexy-looking arms? During his career, he'd been slightly leaner, or at least he'd appeared that way on television and in the press. Did cameras work in reverse for athletes? Make them look smaller than in real life? Or had he added bulk since retiring?

Why did she care? That was the real question.

She must be exhausted if she was eyeballing Domenico Kasa.

"Is that turkey meat reserved for something in particular?" he asked.

Only her *own* sandwich the next day. "No, go ahead," she said with a sigh, reaching into the large double-wide pantry for a loaf of thick-sliced homemade bread. The faster she could help him reach his undesirable carb belly, the better for her overactive, misbehaving hormones.

Domenico Kasa.

Why was she having to remind herself of that?

Even if he hadn't grown into an arrogant jerk, he was her ex-boyfriend's brother. Yuck!

Only so not yuck, she thought as he bent to retrieve the mustard from one of the lower shelves. Nope, nothing yucky about that butt.

She needed to get out of there before lack of sleep combined with lack of sex in recent years made her do something stupid. Like…offer to make his sandwich.

She gathered her things. "Try not to make too much of a mess."

"Heading to bed?" he asked, his tone implying she was a slacker.

She bit back a sarcastic reply about the hour and nodded. "Yes. Good night."

*Just leave.*

"Hey, Adriana."

*Pretend you didn't hear him.*

She paused near the door. "Yeah?"

"Sure you don't want to cool down again in the freezer before you head out? You're looking kinda flushed," he said, an implied smirk in his voice.

Unfortunately, she didn't think the freezer would help. "Good night, Domenico."

His cell phone and hers chimed in unison, and she turned toward him. Reaching into her back pocket she retrieved her phone and opened the text message from Leo at the same moment the smirk died on Domenico's face.

"Oh no," he said.

Reading quickly, Adriana's thoughts echoed his sentiments exactly.

Change of plans. Linda Frank is arriving tomorrow.

# CHAPTER THREE

NOTE TO SELF—*no more late-night snacking.*

*Or at least make sure the kitchen is Adriana-free.*

The only thing erasing the image of her body in her thin, tight-fitting tank top from his mind was the news that Linda Frank was arriving early.

He'd been dreading it before. Now his senses were on high alert as he left the kitchen and scanned the dark resort grounds for anything they may have overlooked—a burnt-out lightbulb since he'd last checked or a loose cobblestone along the paths between the villas. Stilettos and slippery stones did not mix but try telling that to women who insisted on ignoring their warning against skinny, sky-high heels posted multiple times in the guest guide to Kasa de Paradise.

Leo had gone to the mainland the night before and wouldn't rush back, knowing the resort was left in Domenico's capable hands. Irritation about his brother's laid-back attitude surfaced. Leo was the one who said they needed this opportunity, yet all the heavy lifting was left to Domenico.

As usual.

Growing up, Domenico always shouldered the brunt of the responsibilities, despite being the youngest of the brothers. The other two showed eager interest in the day-to-day operations of the family resort business, and their willingness to accept their birthright future without question had appeased their father. Domenico's lack of interest had resulted in his father putting more pressure on him to learn the business, conform, focus…at least until he'd found tennis. Then Leonardo Sr. had redirected the stern all-or-nothing approach towards Domenico's tennis career.

Mario rarely spent time within the hotel walls. He was always off on sourcing trips, attending resort and hotel chain conferences to learn about the latest technologies and promotions. He was a genius when it came to marketing and sourcing expensive wines and delicacies, but he wanted nothing to do with the general running of the resort. He'd already left the island again that day and wouldn't be back until after the reviewer's stay.

When their father got sick, Domenico had quit

his tennis career to move home and care for him in his final days. A choice he'd never regretted. His days as a pro athlete had been numbered, and this venture with his brothers was the future—a continuation of the Kasa legacy.

If only his brothers could take things a little more seriously.

Thank God Adriana had caught the new sense of urgency, grabbing her chef's jacket and getting straight back to work on pre-prepping for the following evening's masquerade event. Another of Leo's great ideas he wasn't here to execute, having gone to the mainland to meet with investors.

At least Adriana was here, a thought that he refused to read too much into. Thrown into the trenches together, they'd reached an unspoken truce that evening. He'd sensed it before leaving her alone in the kitchen, and he was grateful for it.

Maybe it would help him ignore the intense attraction he felt for her. She was gorgeous—always had been. But now she was also sexy as hell. That wild, unruly hair cascading over her shoulders before she'd pulled it back into a tight bun to get to work had been mesmerizing. Adriana's presence could definitely be felt in a room, and normally he had no trouble removing himself from any room she occupied, but that evening, he'd almost hesitated to leave the kitchen.

Remembering the look in her eyes as she'd taken in his bare upper body…the interest reflected there…was unsettling.

How quickly the mood and tension around them had shifted into a sexually charged vibe.

One that couldn't continue.

They had enough to worry about with Linda Frank's arrival. They didn't need to get friendly again. What they'd had as children was in the past, and too much time had passed to rekindle it. They certainly didn't need any stress-fueled attraction developing between them. *That* would be a recipe for disaster.

Domenico had to make sure they weren't alone together often.

Or at all.

Ever.

Reaching his private villa on a secluded end of the resort, Domenico climbed the steps to the door and stepped inside.

The combination of rustic Italian construction with the traditional decor and modern appliances gave the villa a cozy, welcoming vibe. It lacked the pretentiousness of the rest of the resort buildings and held a charm that reminded Domenico of home back in Marina di Corricella, where his mother's family lived and where she insisted their family stay and grow up, even after their family resort chain made them billionaires. She loved their colorful, quaint family home surrounded by lemon groves near Marina Grande, and she rarely left the charming town. Pictures of the town and family photos framed and hung on the walls were the only real decor. He liked things simple.

A breeze from his open patio doors drifted inside, and he could hear the sound of the waves lapping against the private section of beach.

Knowing he'd find it difficult to sleep, he went into the kitchen, poured a glass of scotch over ice, then carried it out onto the deck.

Outside, he sat in his wicker chair and propped his feet up on the railing. He took a swig of the drink as he watched the waves crash along the shore, but despite the breathtaking scenery all around him, he couldn't erase the image of Adriana's flushed cheeks when she'd caught him staring at her breasts.

Nor could he erase the memory of said breasts.

He sighed, ran his uninjured hand over his exhausted, stressed features, then drained the contents of the glass.

He was in for one hell of a week.

Despite going to bed after midnight, Adriana hadn't needed her alarm sounding that morning to wake her. After the best—albeit short—sleep she'd had in probably forever, the sound of the waves crashing on the beach and the birds chirping outside on her private balcony had lured her awake. She stretched in the heavenly bed, enjoying the feel of the cooling bedsheets against her skin and the way the sheer white curtains blew in the breeze coming in through the open ceiling-to-floor windows.

The room was magnificent with its dark wood accents and white adornments. A chaise lounge sat near the open patio doors, with large white pillows making it almost as inviting as the bed. The open-air bathroom had surprised her at first, but taking a shower outside on the secluded deck with the view of the sea and neighboring islands before she'd climbed into bed hours before had been therapeutic. The day's stress had washed away.

Almost completely.

While the reviewer's early arrival had surprised her, she was ready for it. This way, she had little time to overthink what she was doing. Therefore, images of Domenico's gorgeous body had been the only lingering aggravation she'd had to fight as she'd drifted off to sleep.

Avoiding him and keeping him out of her kitchen would be for the best. She didn't like this unfamiliar attraction that had snuck in out of nowhere the night before. She'd known Domenico since they were two years old, and she'd never once thought of him that way. Their bond as children had been friendship. The one they'd nurtured over their teen years through letters had been…a form of adolescent love. But she'd never experienced this deep desire for him. Certainly not in recent years when their only exchanges had contained under-his-breath grunts or looks of obvious disproval.

It was just his body, all sexy and sweaty, combined with her exhaustion that had sent her common sense on a brief hiatus.

But it wouldn't happen again.

Domenico might have retired from tennis, but she suspected his playboy ways were still in practice.

Her cell phone on the night stand rang with an incoming FaceTime call from Isabella, and Adriana smiled as she answered the call. "Hi! How are you?" She sat up in bed and propped up the pillows behind her.

On the screen behind her friend, her three children ran around the kitchen island, screaming and laughing. Isabella winced at the noise. "Counting the days until school starts again."

Adriana laughed. "Hang in there." Her friend certainly had her hands full with her two sons, Berto, six, and Franco, eight, and daughter

Marisella, four. Adriana often envied her friend for her beautiful family but was happy to be Auntie Ada—the nickname affectionately bestowed on her by Marisella, who couldn't say *Adriana*. She wasn't sure yet if she wanted kids of her own. Some days she thought she definitely did, but a babysitting session at Isabella's house always made her realize she wasn't quite ready yet.

On-screen, Isabella disappeared into her kitchen pantry, shut the door and sat on the floor. "Ah, better. How's the island?" She reached for a bag of potato chips and started munching.

"Well, the reviewer is arriving early, and the first event is tonight, so..."

Isabella waved a chip at the screen. "I know you'll crush the review. I'm talking about Leo. Any new sparks flying between you two?"

Adriana shook her head. "Nothing interesting to report. Leo and I are just friends." Which she had repeatedly told her best friend, but Isabella was firmly on Team Reconnect. She thought Adriana was insane for not entertaining the option.

"Fine. Any hot single guests, at least?"

"I've been too busy to notice." Most guests came to Kasa de Paradise in couples, though. Rarely did people drop the extreme amount on a solo trip. And the luxury resort didn't give off bachelor party vibes.

"Come on, Adriana! I'm trying to live vicariously through you!"

"Sorry, guess my life isn't that exciting," she said with a laugh.

"Well, I'm taking the kids to Bellarini's tonight for dinner because if I have to cook one more meal, I'm going to lose it. I'll check in on Alex for you."

"Thank you. I texted him a few times, and he's definitely avoiding me."

Behind Isabella on the screen, the pantry door swung open, and the three kids stared at her.

"Why didn't you tell us we were playing hide-and-seek?" Berto asked.

"You're counting next!" Marisella said with a happy squeal.

Isabella sighed as she closed the bag of potato chips and stood. "And…my vacation is over. Talk soon, bestie."

Adriana blew her friend a kiss as the call disconnected.

Tossing the sheets aside, she climbed out of the bed and walked out onto the deck. The salty breeze in the early morning mist lifting over the island and the quiet tranquility made her sigh. Her day would be crazy preparing the menu for that evening's event, but for a moment, she would enjoy this.

Unfortunately, her appreciation of her luxurious surroundings brought with it the realization of how alone she was in this Mediterranean paradise. On the deck was a table set for two… and a dark wood-trimmed nest chair meant for two…and a private hot tub for two.

She was one.

All alone on a couples' dream vacation.

Not that she'd ever be able to afford luxury like this. Even when the restaurant was doing well, she'd taken a modest salary, living a low-key lifestyle in a one-bedroom condo near the beach. As she was growing up, her parents worked hard at the restaurant to provide a comfortable life and ensure they always had what they needed. Her father was so different from his best friend, Leonardo Kasa Sr., who strived for success and a healthy bank account, but the two men had gonc to the same school as kids and had always been thick as thieves. They respected the other's way of life. Both ambitious and hard-working, the two men had always championed the other's successes. And at their core, family was everything to them both, even if they acted on that priority in different ways. Both wanted to leave a lasting legacy to their families and ensure future generational success…

And at least one of the two men would be proud.

Adriana took in a deep breath of sea air and stared out across the sandy beach below.

A small lizard skirted past her on the deck. Adriana jumped back, then smiled when she saw it scale the wall of the guest suite.

At least she had company.

An hour later, she left her room and walked slowly along the paths through the resort to the main building. The smell of the colorful flowers combined with a faint aroma of citrus was the island's signature scent. It was everywhere, as though spritzed perfectly on the breeze.

The Kasa Island brochure did not boast false promises. This island in the Mediterranean was truly a piece of paradise with its lush natural vegetation, traditional Italian architecture and modern conveniences—it was luxury second to none. And while the serene setting catered to relaxation and rejuvenation of the spirit, the island didn't shy away from extreme pleasure excursions. She could see the zip-line above the trees as she walked and the surfing line in the distant water. There was something for every vacationer.

Beads of sweat gathered on the back of her neck, and she removed her light sweater as she walked. The temperature was already in the eighties, even at that early hour in the morning. Sweating in the hot, humid kitchen that day was going to be her biggest challenge.

That, and *him*.

Tension crept into her shoulders as she saw Domenico on the tennis courts ahead. What was he doing up so early? He'd been up as late as she was. She'd expected—*hoped*—to get a few hours' reprieve from having him lurk around the kitchen and micro-manage her that morning.

A reprieve from drooling over his muscles.

She glanced around the trails. Was there another way to get to the main building without walking past the tennis courts? The signage on the trail pointed in one direction only. The resort's dedication to preserving the native flora and fauna left her no options other than the walking trail she was on.

Maybe Domenico wouldn't notice her. He had his side to her, and he looked focused on the tennis balls coming at him at a crazy speed.

Still, she picked up her pace as she drew closer to the fence around the courts.

Unfortunately, she couldn't help but notice *him*...or rather the chest, arms and stomach that had been etched in her mind all evening. Alone on the court, shirtless in a pair of navy tennis shorts, he battled against a Spinfire Pro, returning lightning-fast balls quicker than she even had time to register them coming. His feet moved with precision back and forth as though anticipating the location of the next one. His broad, muscular shoulders contracted and flexed as he swung and hit each one with an almost violent aggression.

Adriana's mouth went dry. He was hot. Even hotter with the look of determination on his chiseled features, the sweat beading on his forehead and his damp hair pushed back from his face.

She hadn't seen him play in a long time…and never this close.

Shirtless.

Leo had bragged about Domenico's international success over the years, but she'd never been able to get away from the restaurant long enough to attend a match with him. Watching the pro athlete now, there was no question of his skills. Those championships and titles were obviously well-earned. He'd retired from his tennis career at the top of his game to help care for his father when he was sick, but she wondered if he'd really been ready to hang up the racket professionally for good. He was still in top form…

Her gaze settled on his abs flexing and contracting with each breath.

Yep, that form was definitely top-notch.

"You're going to be late for work," Domenico called out, not even glancing her way, never losing focus for the briefest of seconds on the balls whizzing toward him.

Adriana's jaw dropped as she quickly continued along the trail past the tennis courts and out of sight. How did he see her?

Better question—What was she thinking, stopping to watch him play?

Staring at Domenico Kasa shirtless or otherwise was proving to be a pastime that she couldn't afford. Her former childhood friend had somehow gotten to her in the last twenty-four hours in ways she hadn't expected. She'd expected him to be grumpy about her being there, because a scowl was all he ever wore in her presence in recent years. She'd expected him to doubt her abilities in the kitchen, as he'd never once eaten at Bellarini's since she took over as head chef. And she'd expected eventually to be butting heads with him over her menu alterations. But this intense physical attraction to her childhood friend and ex-boyfriend's brother—nope, never, not in a million years.

Therefore, her mission was clear: keep him out of the kitchen and stay away from the tennis courts.

He'd felt Adriana's eyes on him—lingering, drinking him in. Focusing on the ball while being aware of his peripheral surroundings was a situational awareness skill he'd learned as a professional athlete to reduce risk of injury out on the court. Now nothing escaped his notice—whether he wanted it to or not.

Seeing Adriana just now had only given a physical presence to the image he couldn't erase from his mind. He'd even dreamed of her the night before—a delicious dream set in the resort's kitchen that didn't include food. He'd never be able to look at that island countertop the same way again. He felt the front of his shorts grow tight at the mere memory, and he sighed as he stepped out of the line of fire and approached the Spinfire Pro to shut it off.

His cell phone rang as he picked up his towel. He answered the call from Leo, wiping sweat away from his neck and face.

"Hey, bro, when you getting back here?"

The faster he could assign babysitting duties to Leo, the better. Domenico had thought he wanted to supervise Adriana himself that week, but that might not be the best idea. She was turning out to be a distraction he didn't need.

"I'll be back before Linda arrives—just."

"What are you doing over there, anyway?"

"Told you—meeting with a few investors who might be interested in the franchising concept."

Domenico sighed. "Thought we were going to discuss that more." Leo was eager to turn their luxury island concept into a franchise with similar resorts all over the Mediterranean. While Domenico shared his brother's ambition, he wasn't sure he agreed on this particular vision. Kasa de Paradise appealed to guests because of its luxury, but also its uniqueness. If they started duplicating the concept all over Europe, over time not only would it lose its quality, but the lack of rarity would diminish its value.

Mario was still neutral on the idea, so it would basically come down to whichever brother was more persuasive to sway Mario's deciding vote in their favor.

"We are going to discuss it more," Leo said, "but I need to be properly armed for that discussion."

Great.

Domenico sighed as he checked the time on the phone. He needed to shower, dress and head over to the main building for a meeting with the housekeeping staff. "Well, just hurry up, okay? There's still a lot to do."

"I trust you have it covered. How's Adriana doing?"

Domenico's throat constricted at the mention of her, and his "fine" came out as a growl. He cleared his throat and repeated, "Fine."

"You two playing nice?"

Oh, in his dream the night before they were playing *very* nice indeed.

"Everything's cool. Gotta go," he said, disconnecting the call.

He forced a breath as he tucked the phone away and grabbed his things. He needed to get his head on straight and deal with the long to-do list. No more inappropriate thoughts about Adriana or recalling images from his vivid dream the night before.

His cell phone chimed as he left the courts. Retrieving it, he opened a photo message from Leo with the caption, Found this at the old house while looking for some financial paperwork.

Domenico's heart skipped as he saw a photo of the five of them as kids—Leo, Mario, Alex, Adriana and himself—on the beach. He and Adriana were in the middle, arms around one another. She was smiling at the camera, her dark hair blowing in the breeze behind her, but his gaze was directed on her. He sighed as he caught the look on his preteen face.

So maybe this attraction to her wasn't coming a hundred percent out of nowhere.

Wonderful. Just wonderful.

# CHAPTER FOUR

SHE REMEMBERED THAT summer day on the beach near the Kasa family home, but Adriana didn't recall posing for the group photo she was staring at on her phone in the text message from Leo—nor did she remember ever seeing Domenico look at her the way he was in the image.

Her chest was tight as she zoomed in on the picture so that it was only the two of them in the frame. She was smiling at the camera—almost as though she'd been laughing at something right before the flash went off. No doubt it was something Domenico had said. Years ago he used to make her laugh until she peed. He used to be funny. Odd how that memory struck her now—she'd forgotten that about him.

But it was his expression that had her heart racing. It was, dare she say it, lovestruck? As lovestruck as a preteen boy could be...

A timer chimed on the counter behind her. She sighed as she tucked the cell phone into her apron pocket and got back to work.

Linda Frank was scheduled to arrive in three hours, and Leo had planned a resort tour for her that afternoon, so she only had another hour to prep for the evening before she'd have to clean up.

She slid a multislicer through stacked sheets of pasta, then carefully dropped the pasta strands into the deep fryer. They sizzled for a minute before she removed them and dipped them in a mixture of sugar, cinnamon and cocoa, savoring the sweet aroma as she worked. After setting them on a tray, she repeated the process.

Galani were one of her guilty pleasures, and they were the perfect bite-sized dessert to complement the sweet tasting menu for that evening's masquerade-themed party.

She shook her head. If anyone could pull off such an elaborate event, it was the resort's entertainment staff. She'd caught a glimpse of the decor and setup in the lower section of the main building that was curtained off in preparation for the event. It already looked magnificent. Dark, rich colors like emerald green and deep red for the velvety textured fabrics of the curtains and furniture coverings added a layer of mystery while in contrast, candlesticks and mirrors in metallics like silver and gold created a striking, regal presence in the room. Pearl beads, long dark feathers and masks of various dark metallics completed the design with an impressive flair.

The five-course sit-down dinner menu that Chef Dubois had planned, however, was less impressive, so Adriana was making adjustments.

She picked up one of the pasta strips, bit into it and closed her eyes as the flavors of cinnamon and chocolate danced on her tongue. “Mmm.”

“Are you preparing the food or eating it?”

Only Domenico could ruin this near-sensual experience for her.

He might have had a crush on her when they were kids, if the photo could be believed, but that wasn’t the expression he wore on his face now as she opened her eyes.

Licking the powdered sugar from her lip, she said, “Chefs need to sample their creations before serving them to guests.” Reluctantly she held out the tray. “Care to try one?”

“Galani?”

She nodded, avoiding looking at him too long. He’d obviously showered since his morning workout on the tennis court. Dressed in a white collared shirt and tan khaki pants, he looked cool and refreshed—not at all bothered by the intense humidity that had the few tendrils of her hair that escaped her bun curling at the base of her neck.

He looked tempted, but shook his head as he

patted his flat stomach. "Someone told me I needed to watch my weight," he said, glancing around the kitchen and surveying the various trays of hors d'oeuvres and sweet bite-sized delicacies. "Is this everything for tonight's event?" He frowned.

She hadn't cleared her new adjustments with anyone, and there'd be no more avoiding the conversation. "Yes. I made some changes to the menu," she said confidently. She refused to let him shake her on this decision.

*"Some?"*

She scanned the rows of appetizers on the counters. "Okay, a lot of changes. I changed the whole thing." She may have gone a tad too far. "Chef Dubois had a full sit-down five-course dinner planned, but given the nature of the event, I thought a wide selection of finger foods would be more appropriate."

"Our guests like to eat," Domenico said, looking mildly panicked. He fingered his open collar at his neck.

So maybe not so unaffected by the heat. Or was it her and her decision-making causing him to break out into a sweat?

"Yes, but they will be wearing masks and evening gowns," she muttered, standing her ground. "Bite-sized pieces and things that are consumed best at room temperature is a more appropriate way to go. Not to mention the waitstaff will have a much easier time serving."

A stress line appeared on Domenico's forehead, and she could see a slight throbbing in a darkening vein at his temple. The man was seriously stressed over this.

"Chef Dubois didn't think so," he said.

"You fired Chef Dubois."

He checked his watch, then massaged his forehead as though hoping to ease his frustration. "It's after noon. I guess we're stuck with this."

Stuck?

Adriana's teeth clenched so tightly together, her jaws hurt. "Just because the portion sizes are small doesn't mean they're not delicious." She scanned the trays. Selecting a garlic stuffed mushroom, she approached and extended it to him. "Try this."

Domenico shook his head, his nose wrinkled in disgust. "I'm not a fan of mushrooms. It's the text..."

Adriana reached up and stuffed it into his open mouth.

Domenico's eyes widened in shock at first at the gesture. Then his expression changed as he slowly chewed. Changed from surprise to consideration to an obvious look of approval...and dare she hope...enjoyment?

She smiled. "What were you saying about texture?"

He swallowed the appetizer and nodded at the row of them on the tray with a suspicious look. "Those are mushrooms? They didn't taste slimy at all."

"Not all mushrooms are the same. Some are soft and meaty..."

His gaze locked with hers. "But most are slimy...even the ones that don't appear so at first glance."

"I think you are wrongly accusing all mushrooms of the same crime without trying the full spectrum. Choose the right one and you could be pleasantly surprised," she said, feeling her pulse race in her veins.

He was too close, they were too alone, and she couldn't remember what they were talking about anymore. When he stepped toward her, she couldn't be sure whose hands reached out first, but in a confusing instant, his were on her waist and hers were pressed against his chest. His head bent to the side and his gaze locked with hers as his lips moved closer.

"Is that the case only with mushrooms, or are there more surprises in your kitchen?" he muttered, his lips grazing hers.

She swallowed hard as her fingers gripped the

light, soft fabric of his shirt. "You tell me," she said, pressing her body into him.

His mouth crushed hers then, and her breath caught at the intense passion and desire she'd never have guessed he could possess. Gone was the rigid, reserved exterior. Right now, he was open and inviting…and dangerous. Her arms went higher to encircle his neck as she moved even closer, deepening the kiss, her tongue exploring his mouth as his desperately searched hers.

He smelled so good, like the salty breeze combined with the sweet scent of the island, mixed with a hint of expensive cologne. She could breathe that delicious scent in all day. He turned his head to the other side, his hands gripping tighter on her waist as he ran his tongue along her bottom lip, then grabbed it between his teeth to bite gently, before pulling away.

Her eyes flew open in time to see his look of remorse as he released her.

Her hand flew to her mouth, and neither of them spoke.

They didn't have to. The kiss had said far too much already.

Still, he stood there, staring at her…expecting what? An apology? An explanation? He'd be waiting a long time for either.

"That can't happen again," he finally said.

"*You* kissed *me*," she said, fighting to control her thundering heartbeat echoing loudly in her ears.

He guffawed. "As if you weren't begging me to."

Adriana mouth gaped. "You can't be serious. Why on earth would I want to kiss you? You're arrogant and rude and judgmental…and…" She searched for more insults. "You're prejudiced against all fungi."

Domenico took a step toward her, his gaze burning into hers with the same intensity she'd felt in his kiss. "Why would *I* want to kiss *you*? You're loud and uncompromising. You've been here less than twenty-four hours, and you've destroyed a perfectly good menu…"

"*Fixed* an inappropriate menu," she corrected him, taking a step closer, her hands on her hips.

"That's a matter of opinion," he muttered, moving even closer until they were toe to toe—inches apart.

The heat sizzling between them rivaled any coming from the kitchen appliances. Their gazes locked in a tension-filled standoff. She raised her chin an inch more.

"So, you're saying you didn't like the mushroom?"

He hesitated for a long time. Then the heavy exhale that escaped him blew her hair away from her face. "The mushroom was an unexpected pleasure..." he said carefully as one does when they fear their words could somehow be used against them in court. "But one that I don't plan on indulging in recklessly again."

A hint of a smile played on her lips at the tiny victory. "But you liked it?"

Domenico shook his head in slight annoyance that he was giving her the win, turned and headed toward the door. "It might be the best thing I've ever had in my mouth."

Adriana's smile was wide as she watched him walk out. Then her hand flew to her lips, where his had just been, and her smile faded.

What the hell was that?

Without a doubt, the best kiss of her life.

Domenico paced the dock an hour later, waiting for the *Passage to Paradise*.

He had to convince Leo that Adriana was a mistake. Having her at the resort this week had already been a gamble. Now it was a personal liability. That kiss in the kitchen had been an impulsive, stupid move, and he should never have let it happen, but the woman got under his skin in ways no one ever had. The kiss had been almost about teaching her a lesson.

*What* lesson, he didn't know. And unfortunately, it had backfired.

Instead of showing her who was boss, it told him he wasn't it.

She had to go.

His lack of self-control around her would make this week even more tension-filled and stressful. Added complications were the last thing they needed with so much on the line. A good review from Linda Frank could turn Kasa de Paradise into one of the world's top travel destinations. A negative one could sink them.

This woman was brutal. And she could afford to be. She was sought-after, and resorts asked her to review them—they essentially gave her the power she wielded.

The Kasa brothers were giving her that power.

Because...they believed in what they'd achieved here through dedication, hard work, commitment...and focus.

Now, after that kiss, Domenico's focus was destroyed.

The sous-chef and the rest of the kitchen team would have to step up and prove themselves. Now was their time to shine. Maybe they'd discover a new head chef.

Seeing the boat approach, he watched as it sailed into the harbor and carefully docked next to the pier.

"Good afternoon, Mr. Domenico," Jon said, hopping off and securing the line.

"Hey, Jon," he said distractedly, turning his attention to his brother as Leo disembarked. "We need to rethink this whole Adriana thing."

Leo shook his head and shot Domenico a silent warning before reaching behind him to extend a hand to a tiny dark-haired woman in a tan skirt and white blouse.

It was too late.

Domenico's palms were instantly covered in sweat, and his stomach did somersaults.

"Domenico, this is Linda Frank from *Travel Island* magazine. Linda, I'd like you to meet my brother and business partner, Domenico."

"Hi, welcome..." This wasn't the way he'd wanted to meet the woman, all frazzled and with the taste of Adriana still on his lips, but here they were. He extended a hand toward her, and she eyed him carefully as she shook it. Her hand was as cool as an ice cube.

They were in trouble.

Why was she staring at him like that? Could she somehow sense that he'd just been kissing their temporary chef in the resort kitchen? Was her reviewer spidey sense picking up on a potential sexual harassment claim?

His heart was pounding so loud he didn't hear Leo until he repeated himself. "Dom, you can let go now."

Right. He was holding her hand hostage in his. He released her. "Sorry about that."

"You're the tennis pro—Domenico Kasa, right?"

That depends. Did she like tennis? He hesitated.

"He is. The one and only. And he usually can speak for himself, but he's obviously starstruck," Leo said smoothly, shooting him a look that said *pull it together*.

Domenico cleared his throat. "Yes, I can. Apologies, Ms. Frank. I was expecting you on a later boat."

She nodded. "Guilty. I like to spring unexpected surprises on my hosts. Speaking of which, I have to say, that boat ride was unexpectedly smooth, and the view coming in through the narrows was breathtaking," she told him with a smile.

So far so good. But Domenico wasn't fooled. Beneath the smile and compliment was a woman with piercing, perceptive eyes just looking for one wrong move, one slipup. Her job was to find the issues, the problems, the reasons guests might spend their money elsewhere. Her readers expected the very best if she recommended a resort, and she took that position of service to the tourism industry very seriously.

"Thank you. We pride ourselves on giving

guests the best of luxury from the moment they book with us," he said, taking her bag as they walked along the dock toward the main building.

She nodded. "I did take the liberty of trying out the online registration system under a false name. I have to say again that the process was as smooth and easy as promised. The online concierge was very helpful and knowledgeable," she said.

Each member of the staff from the gardeners to the bartenders completed their three-month intensive training course on every aspect of the resort before they stepped onto the island. It was a process their father had always insisted on for every hotel they opened within the family's former chain. All staff needed to have a basic working knowledge of everyone else's position—not to step in to do it, but to encourage mutual respect among the staff. No job was insignificant in running a resort, and Leonardo Sr. treated everyone with the utmost courtesy and consideration. They hired only the best, and they treated them as the VIP staff they were.

"We take our staff selection process seriously," he said.

"I reviewed your staffing policies, and they are quite inclusive and unique."

"Unique in a good way?" Leo was cheeky enough to ask.

Linda just winked at him.

"So, this is the main building," Leo said a moment later when they reached it and entered. "As you can see, check in is fully automated with the kiosks." He gestured to a row of four check-in machines in the large, open-air foyer where they hosted nightly entertainment with a bar, a grand piano and comfortable lounge chairs and tables. A laid-back yet classy area for guests to relax and unwind at the end of the evening.

Linda moved closer to a kiosk. "In my experience, this can sometimes slow the process. Guests aren't all tech-savvy. Losing the personal touch of guest attendants in favor of technology isn't always progress in the tourism industry."

Right there. He knew not to let his guard down at that smile and wink of hers. Luckily the Kasa brothers were prepared for that particular criticism.

"We totally agree. Our father always said that guests will forgive just about anything as long as they are greeted with professionalism and courtesy," Leo said.

"Your father was a smart man," Linda said. "I had the pleasure of reviewing one of his hotels. Unfortunately it was later in the chain's lifespan, and some things had deteriorated."

Like their father's health. Without Leonardo Kasa Sr. at the helm, the hotel board had started to make decisions around him—decisions that cut costs, but also weakened the Kasa hotel chain. By the time the brothers sold it, it was no longer up to the standard of family pride they'd grown up in.

And they'd seen Linda's review—one that would have been detrimental had they not already closed the deal to sell the hotel chain. Their previous experience with Linda had been one of the reasons Domenico had been wary of this idea, but Mario and Leo insisted this was a great way for the Kasa hotel brand to redeem themselves.

"I commend your decision to sell the chain and open Kasa de Paradise. Smart move, though I understand it might not have been an easy one," she said.

Leo nodded. "Thank you. Our father gave his blessing before he passed, and I think we've done him proud."

"Back to the system," Domenico said, the conversation getting a tad too personal for his liking. "When we put it in, we designed it with guest ease of use in mind. Therefore it's a simple swipe of the armband provided to our guests on the boat. Give it a try," Domenico said, nodding to the armband Linda wore.

Linda extended her arm over the scanner. Immediately the screen lit up with her personal reservation info.

"Welcome to Kasa de Paradise," a smiling guest attendant greeted her on-screen. "Get ready to smile in 3…2…1…"

Linda smiled, and the camera took her picture.

"Thank you," the on-screen host said. "Now you may remove your armband. Enjoy your stay with us."

Linda grinned as she removed the armband. "That was clever. I was going to dock you points for this annoying thing."

Leo took the armband from her. "We know," he said with a wink.

Linda eyed him. "Okay, but from an environmental standpoint, aren't the armbands just a waste of time and useless now?"

Domenico shook his head. "Nope. They are recycled and recalibrated at the front desk."

Linda nodded slowly. "Okay, I like it…but there's still the element of the personal touch…"

"Your drink, Ms. Frank," a voice said right on cue behind them.

He loved their staff.

Even Linda's unpredictable early arrival hadn't shaken them. The moment the three of them had entered, the staff had been discreetly on alert. And the best part was, this wasn't for show. Any and all guests received the same treatment.

Linda laughed as she turned toward the young server with the pressed Kasa de Paradise uniform and sincere smile. "Thank you," she said as she accepted the sweet-and-sour martini with olives from the tray and took a sip.

Domenico and Leo waited for her reaction.

"This is…good. Real good."

Domenico's shoulders relaxed slightly, and Leo's confident smile was back in place.

"You guys have impressed me so far, but don't rest easy. This is only the beginning of my stay," Linda said, taking another sip of the drink.

Domenico nodded. "We wouldn't think of it."

Behind Linda's back, Leo was giving a thumbs-up. While Domenico was just as relieved that the initial meeting had gone well, he knew Linda meant what she said.

She'd only been there ten minutes. There was still plenty of time for something to go wrong.

His chest tightened as he remembered the steamy kiss in the kitchen. Adriana's lips on his had felt like sinful indulgence. The taste of her had rivaled the sweetness of the galani and the delicacy of the mushroom. Her hands gripping his shirt and the way she'd pressed her body into him. It had nearly knocked him on his butt. Had definitely thrown him off his game.

Still plenty of time for something *else* to go wrong.

* * *

"See. Told you things would be fine. You need to relax," Leo said an hour later in their office as he collapsed into the chair behind the desk and stifled a yawn.

"Relax? There's a high-profile reviewer touring the facility and interviewing our staff as we speak." Domenico stood at the window, where he could see Linda moving throughout the resort grounds with her tablet. After he'd toured her through the facilities, she'd insisted on a solo tour. Every time she paused too long or jotted something down, his heart raced.

What was she making notes about?

He took his phone out of his pocket and snapped a photo, then zoomed in on the tablet.

Too blurry. He couldn't read anything.

"You've made sure that everything was perfect, so quit stressing. Besides, there's nothing we can do now." Leo stood and picked up his golf putter. He approached the mini-putt green in the corner of the office, rotated his shoulders, lined up the shot, then sent the golf ball sliding into the hole. "By the way, what were you going to say about Adriana earlier on the dock?"

*She's both a fantastic chef and kisser.*

Heat crept up Domenico's neck as guilt washed over him. It was too late to replace her without Linda noticing the switch, so now he just had to deal with it. Deal with her and having that temptress of a body around the resort all week. And deal with this sudden attraction that, according to the nostalgic photo, might not actually be so sudden. It still baffled him. Had he completely blocked out any feelings he'd once had for Adriana? Was it some kind of trauma self-preservation thing? They'd been great friends. Then that connection had grown over the years through their correspondence… but then BAM! He'd come home from a tennis tour, excited to see her, explore what their young emotions could be for one another, and she was dating his brother!

Talk about a punch to the nuts.

There was no denying he'd liked her back then and was attracted to her now…and it was problematic.

"Nothing," he said. "We're stuck with her." He ran a hand through his hair and checked his watch. "I need to shower and change."

"I had guest services deliver your masquerade outfit to your villa."

Right. These events weren't only for the guests. Leonardo Sr. always said that guests had more fun and embraced the theme nights more when the hotel staff and management teams also participated. He always treated guests as family at his hotels, and families ate, drank and laughed together.

Domenico wasn't totally opposed, but this event in particular seemed a little challenging. At least it did now after Adriana had raised some good points. "You sure we should be trying a new event this week?"

"It's already on the calendar. Guests are looking forward to it," Leo said, realigning his shot. He swung and hit the ball. It went a fraction of an inch right of the hole.

Domenico sighed. "Are you going to play all day, or are you actually going to do some work?"

Leo grinned. "Haven't decided yet."

Domenico shook his head as he left the office. His brother was one of the best business minds he knew, and he was the success behind Kasa de Paradise, but if he didn't get serious about his responsibilities soon, he could also be their downfall. Leo believed that fate played a large part in life and that things always worked out as they should. A belief he'd inherited from their mother. Domenico was more of a take-charge-of-one's-fate kind of guy. Point your destiny where you wanted it to go, rather than following with blind faith.

At his villa, he headed around to the outside shower. Removing his khakis and shirt, he turned on the gentle waterfall stream and surveyed the view around him as he stepped under the water.

This place was magical. Guests arrived here stressed, overworked, exhausted and left feeling rejuvenated, refreshed and reinvigorated. He was proud of what they'd built—a true paradise in a chaotic, unsettled world.

After the reviewer's visit, he'd take a week off, give himself the opportunity to unwind a little and enjoy the perks of the island himself.

He closed his eyes as the cool water ran down his back. An image of Adriana immediately came to mind. Out of all the challenges that week posed, being around her was the toughest.

Why had he kissed her?

And why was he desperate to do it again? It was a mistake, one he couldn't repeat. She was currently an employee, a long-time family friend, and she'd always be Leo's ex.

Off-limits for so many reasons, but unfortunately, whenever someone told him he couldn't have something, it only made him want it more.

Maybe that's all it was. The fact that Adriana was the last woman on earth he could have was making him want her.

Staying away from her wasn't an option, since he was determined to make sure she didn't do anything to jeopardize their review. He was just going to have to learn to control the intense, irrational attraction he had to her.

It was just for a week.

He could keep his hands and lips off his brother's ex-girlfriend—a woman he might have been harboring unacknowledged, buried feelings for since he was a kid—for that long, couldn't he?

Absolutely.

# CHAPTER FIVE

ADRIANA COLLAPSED ONTO her bed several hours later. All of the food was prepped for that evening's event, and she had an hour before she had to get back there to oversee the kitchen.

She'd heard the buzz around the resort. Linda Frank was there. The entire staff was vibrating on a higher intensity, and the general mood of Kasa de Paradise had shifted into another level of professionalism and hospitality. The reviewer hadn't been into the kitchen yet, but Adriana was on high alert. This review meant everything. Not only to the Kasa resort's success, but to her own. The food would be highly critiqued as part of the review, and the chance to have her culinary skills praised in such a high-profile magazine by a well-respected reviewer had her functioning on adrenaline alone.

She couldn't mess this up.

She was a skilled and proficient chef. Professional and commanding in the kitchen. She demanded excellence and delivered the same.

And as long as she could keep from kissing Domenico Kasa again, everything would be fine.

She rolled over and muffled a loud groan into her heavenly pillow.

The kiss should have been horrible. It should have made her want to gag. It was Domenico freaking Kasa, the most arrogant, annoying man on earth and a childhood friend. Not to mention her ex-boyfriend's brother. That alone should have made Domenico a nonsexual inanimate object in her mind—like one of the tiki torches illuminating the island trails. She should not have enjoyed it, and it certainly shouldn't have played on repeat in her mind while she'd worked.

She'd kept expecting him to come back into the kitchen for either another round or to explain his actions away. Which she'd been anticipating—or hoping for? She wasn't sure.

He was technically her boss for that week, but it had been clear by the look on his face when he'd pulled away that he hadn't felt one bit in control. That kiss had been as unexpected to him as it had been to her.

Therefore, it didn't have to mean anything, right? Just a little glitch. A little slipup in the heat of an argument. Two attractive, hot-blooded, passionate people who let a moment in time sweep them away.

That was it. No more. No less.

She wasn't sure she bought all that she was telling herself, but it calmed her for the moment.

She rolled onto her back and stared at the ceiling. The breeze blowing in through her open patio doors held the same sweet floral island fragrance. The soft bedsheets and pillows beneath her were comfy and soothing to her tired body. She closed her eyes.

For just a second… She would not fall asleep.

Loud knocking made her jump what felt like seconds later. Her eyes flew open, and her heart raced as she sat up. The room was darker, and a glance outside the patio doors revealed dusk had settled over the island.

Where had the sun gone?

Panic gripped her as she glanced at the clock. Seven thirty?

She'd fallen asleep. An hour nap had felt like six seconds. She jumped up off the bed and peeked through the hole in the door.

Dom.

Oh no. What was he doing here? Another make-out sesh?

No, that would be stupid. Sexy, fun and hot, but definitely stupid.

She fixed her hair as she opened the door. "Hey, I was just going to start heading back." She caught a glimpse of her reflection in the mirror across the hall. After a quick sponge bath and makeup application. She was a frizzy, sweaty mess after all day in the kitchen.

"Good I caught you then," he said, entering the room. "I was bringing you this." He took a big white box from behind his back and extended it toward her.

"What is it?"

"It's for the event tonight," he said as she carried it to the bed.

She removed the lid, and her stomach twisted. A deep red satin dress and matching mask were inside along with a pair of red velvet ballet flats. "Nope. I'm staff. I'm not here on vacation." She needed to get to the event to make sure everything went well—food-wise. She wasn't dressing up and participating.

He shook his head. "You're part of the executive staff. We all participate in the theme nights," he said with a sigh as though he wasn't thrilled about that job requirement either. "It's part of our promise to our guests, so technically it's part of your job."

She swallowed hard as she stared at the outfit he expected her to wear. "Overseeing everything will be challenging in this..."

"The food is already done, and we have waitstaff who will be doing all the work. This is where you get to enjoy some of the perks of employment with Kasa de Paradise," he said tightly.

Was that what this was about? Was he trying to sell her on the idea of working here? Working for them?

No way. Domenico would never hire her full-time.

Unless that kiss earlier today had meant something…

The look of lust reflected in his dark eyes earlier that day plagued her. What had started as an argument-fueled embrace had quickly turned into a full-fledged passionate kiss. But that would only make him more eager for her to leave, right?

Definitely not a reason to want her to stay.

It wasn't as though they could act on whatever crazy chemistry existed between them. She was Leo's ex, and she would never do that to him. And Domenico was loyal to his family. He had to be making the same no-repeat vow she was.

It was in the past; they couldn't change it.

Would she if she could?

Dom checked his watch. "Just hurry. Event starts in thirty minutes."

Adriana nodded as he turned to leave. Then she frowned. "Hey, where did this come from, anyway?"

"The boutique shop on site. We had these ordered in so that guests wouldn't have to bring themed event clothing along on vacation."

She eyed the dress. "How did you know what size?"

Dom's gaze swept over her seductively from head to toe. "It will fit," he said huskily, letting his gaze linger on her a moment longer before stalking toward the door and letting himself out.

She sighed, staring at the gown with its low plunging neckline and high side slit. Hardly suitable for being on the job. What was Dom thinking?

She couldn't wear this.

Unfortunately, she didn't think she had much choice. Nothing she'd packed would fit the dress code requirement for that evening…and it was gorgeous. Exactly her taste and style. How did Dom know her so well?

What was he thinking bringing such a revealing dress? Wanting to see her in it, perhaps?

She shook her head, hoping to reactivate common sense. It didn't matter. She was here to do a job. Nothing more.

She certainly wasn't here to get caught up in a problematic situationship with a paradise billionaire.

"Do you like my dress?"

At that moment, Pricilla Conway could be standing there in a full ski suit or stark naked and Domenico wouldn't know. His gaze was locked on another dress entering the main building. Vibrant red with gold trim that dipped in a sharp low V at the bodice, made of satiny, almost transparent fabric that clung to a sexy pair of hips.

He was finally grateful he was wearing this stupid mask. Now if the resort's CCTV cameras caught him in the act, no one would immediately identify him as the one who tried to rip it off her.

"Excuse me for a second, Mrs. Conway," he said, still not looking at her and heading toward Adriana.

Behind the red-and-gold mask, Adriana's emerald eyes were blazing fire when her gaze met his.

She looked like one burning flame from head to toe. One he was safest not to touch. Yet the temptation to run his hand along the thin, silky fabric—down her sides, over her tiny waist—to caress the shapely curves of her hips was so strong he shoved his hands deep into his pants pockets.

He shook his head. *Focus.* "Things are running late. Food should have been out ten minutes ago."

"I just stopped by the kitchen." She nodded across the room. "There are the servers now."

Their waitstaff, dressed in black tuxedos and simple black masks, were rolling out the hot plates of appetizers and finger foods she'd prepared earlier that day.

"Good," he said.

Adriana too sighed in relief, and her chest rose and fell, causing his eyes to immediately drop to her breasts. Earlier that day he'd vowed she wouldn't be a distraction. He'd given himself a firm talking-to, and he'd had no intentions of allowing himself to be caught off guard by another impulsive moment of weakness with her. And yet when he'd seen this dress in the boutique window, he'd known it was made for her. He'd been in an almost trancelike state when he'd bought it and delivered it to her room. And now he was staring at those breasts and contemplating kissing her in front of the room full of people.

"Your friend is giving me the evil eye," Adriana said with a nod behind him, snapping his attention back to her face.

He didn't have to turn around to know who she was talking about. "That would be Mrs. Pricilla Conway. She's a little territorial." And the ultimate antidote to the impeding, inconvenient arousal forming in his pants. Maybe having Pricilla around this week was a good thing after all.

"And terrifying," Adriana whispered, moving to stand to his side, out of Pricilla's daggers.

Domenico couldn't suppress a laugh at the all

too accurate description. "Yes, she is. I wouldn't turn my back on her for very long."

"Thanks for the warning."

Their gazes met and held beneath their masks. The look in her eyes was puzzling and he longed for the ability to read her mind. What was she thinking? Had she thought about their kiss that day as much as he had? Would she address it? Should he? He was technically her boss, so he should say something.

"Adriana..."

But what exactly?

That what had happened in the kitchen had been a reckless, impulsive act that couldn't happen again and meant absolutely nothing? Not exactly the truth. That he was sorry that he'd taken advantage? Again, not entirely true. She'd been just as into that kiss as he'd been. Arrogance would hazard to say even more so. Again—a lie. He was really into it.

"Adriana," he started again.

She stared at him expectantly.

Those emerald eyes behind that mask were intoxicating. Like, wipe all coherent thoughts from his brain intoxicating.

All he could think about was how much he'd like to take a pair of scissors to that fabric. An image of the satin falling away from her body made him shift uncomfortably, arousal reinitiated.

"I should go check to see if Linda has arrived yet. Don't forget you're here to do a job as well," he told Adriana stiffly before stalking away.

He needed to pull it together. Yes, she was gorgeous. Yes, he was attracted to her. But she was off-limits.

Yeah, that forbidden fruit thing only made the whole thing hotter.

"Hey…" a voice purred to this left as he made his way across the room.

He suppressed a sigh. If the sight of his brother and Adriana talking and laughing didn't kill him, Pricilla was sure to be the death of him. "Hi, Mrs. Conway. You look stunning," he said, taking her extended hand and allowing her to turn slowly, displaying everything she'd put on display that evening in a black, too-tight leather dress. The silver zipper that ran along the front promised easy access, and the black leather mask she wore looked more appropriate for a BDSM session. Domenico scanned the ballroom. "Where is Mr. Conway?"

Her seductive grin faded. "He found his true love already," she said, nodding toward the older man chatting up one of the servers as he sampled the hors d'oeuvres.

"Well, I apologize to have to rush off again,

but I need to find the resort reviewer…" He scanned the room. These stupid costumes made it hard to identify her.

"Ms. Frank? She's lovely."

Pricilla's words made him pause. "You've met her?"

She nodded, linking her arm through his and picking an imaginary piece of lint from his suit jacket, where her hand lingered on his chest. "Yes. She was poolside for a little while just before dinner."

He hated using Mrs. Conway as a potential ally, but he was dying to know. "Did she say how she was enjoying her stay so far?"

Pricilla leaned closer and whispered, "I think you need to be more concerned about how the guests are enjoying their stay… After all, happy guests make for a great review, right?" The sultry smile that curled on her lips didn't reach her eyes. Instead, there was a hint of—a threat?

Domenico swallowed hard. Happy guests he could do. Pimping himself out to this woman was where he drew the line. Not at his resort. Review on the line or not, he refused to be someone's boy toy. "Your husband looks very happy enjoying the food. Perhaps you should join him." He removed her hand from his arm and walked away, feeling her burning gaze on the back of his neck.

Of course the woman with the biggest mouth on the island had to be interested in him. This was not good.

If Pricilla didn't get what she wanted, no one would.

# CHAPTER SIX

SWEAT POOLED ON Adriana's lower back beneath the satin fabric as she watched Linda Frank survey the hors d'oeuvres circling the room on the trays later that evening. The event had started to wind down. Maybe all of the full-flavored, decadent options hadn't been the right decision. From her perch near the buffet table, she watched as the reviewer, dressed in a teal-green sequined dress and matching mask, reached for a glass of champagne from a serving tray instead.

Why wasn't she eating anything? She'd passed on the stuffed mushrooms, the mini-quiches… She looked to be contemplating the galani, and Adriana held her breath.

Nope. Linda shook her head and sipped the champagne.

Fantastic. The woman barely ate. Or were the choices not up to her standards?

Adriana bit her lower lip as she watched Linda drain the contents of the glass and check her watch. A moment later, she was waving goodbye to several of the staff.

She was leaving? She hadn't tasted anything.

"She ordered a full sampling plate to go," a voice whispered near her ear. She jumped. Then goose bumps surfaced all over her skin.

Her heart raced and she barely comprehended the words as she turned to look at Domenico just as he removed his mask.

"What?" she asked, reaching behind her to do the same.

"The servers told me that she ordered a sampling plate of all of the hors d'oeuvres and desserts to be packaged and brought to her room. Something about a fasting diet—she doesn't eat after seven p.m."

Adriana released a sigh of relief but then frowned. "Well, she can't be eating my dinners as breakfast. Dinner service will start at six this week. Guests will have to adjust their schedules accordingly."

She expected pushback or at least an argument, but surprisingly, Domenico nodded. "Already told the activity staff to make the adjustment and send out the revised schedule first thing in the morning. Dinner will still run until ten but start an hour earlier."

She struggled to hide her surprise at his cooperation as she struggled with the tie of the mask. What the…? It seemed to be knotted…

Domenico stepped forward and nodded toward it. "Having trouble?"

She nodded.

He moved closer and reached for her hands, lowering them out of the way. Then he leaned closer, peering over the top of her head and reaching for the mask ties. Her face was inches from his chest, and the scent of his expensive cologne filled her senses.

He smelled good. How? In this heat, he smelled fresh and…like a man who could tear her apart. Like a man she'd readily allow to tear her apart.

Her heart raced. She felt his fingers touch the back of her head as he pulled at the knot in the mask. "It's tangled in your hair. Stay still," he said.

Her knees nearly gave out at the simple command.

*Stay still.* Yes, sir. Any other positions he'd like her in?

What was in that cologne?

Domenico released her hair and moved away from her. "You're free."

"Thank you," she said, her gaze locked with his.

Domenico checked his watch. "I have an

early lesson tomorrow…so guess I should call it a night." He hesitated, glancing at Adriana. "I mean, unless you want to…grab a drink?" His gaze searched hers, and she didn't know what answers he was looking for. His close proximity and the tantalizing scent of him moments before had created a whirlwind of turmoil through her. She wanted to get away from him and these unwanted, unexpected emotions…but at the same time, she would rather have a drink with him.

"Never mind. You should probably get some sleep," Domenico said abruptly in her long silence. "Breakfast prep starts at five a.m.," he said, the familiar coolness and note of authority reminding her he was technically her boss this week.

Her expression hardened. So that's what his expression was about—he was waiting for her to do the responsible thing and call it a night? Testing her work ethic?

"You're right—I have an early start tomorrow. Tonight was a good beginning, but we want to make sure we keep impressing Ms. Frank." She needed it just as much as they did.

Domenico nodded, and Adriana hesitated a fraction of a second before leaving the main building and descending the stairs. She glanced behind her and waited. Several guests exited, and she smiled at them as they passed. “Night,” she said.

She waited another minute. No sign of Domenico.

Of course not. What was wrong with her?

She headed toward the trail to her guest room. Once she rounded the first bend in the trail, she removed her flats and continued barefoot toward her suite.

The sound of the waves on the beach and the palm trees swaying in the breeze truly made this a paradise. It was easy to forget that they were such a short distance from the mainland, a short boat ride back to all the troubles and worries that awaited her there. She couldn’t fault Leo for his laid-back, carefree demeanor. This island life had a way of making her forget that she was there to work.

At one time, all of this had been offered to her.

A lizard scurried past her on the trail, and she laughed as she sidestepped him. “You almost got crushed, little guy,” she said as he scurried into the brush.

“Nah, they’re pretty fast.”

Domenico’s voice drifting from the shadows nearby made her heart race. She could barely see him—just his silhouette illuminated by the outdoor trail lights. What was he doing there? And why was she so happy that he was?

"How did you get here so fast?" she asked as she approached him.

"Island cruiser," he said, gesturing to a small vehicle parked on the sand. It looked like a go-cart with off-roading tires.

"I thought you were heading off to bed." Her heart pounded steadily in her chest.

"I had second thoughts about that drink and thought maybe you would too," he said, walking toward her. He was still in his tuxedo, but the tie hung loose around his neck, and the shirt was unbuttoned down his chest. "Join me for one on the beach?" he asked, holding up a bottle of expensive champagne and two plastic champagne glasses.

She swallowed hard. They couldn't be sneaking around the island at night alone for secret champagne rendezvous. Not that this was a rendezvous.

"Do you want to change first…or…?" Domenico asked. His gaze took in her body in the gown, and the lust-filled expression was undeniable.

Staying in the dress it was.

She shook her head. "It's surprisingly comfortable."

Domenico laughed as he nodded toward the path down to the water.

Adriana followed him to the beach, then

scanned the sand beneath them. This part of the beach wasn't swimmable, so there were no beach chairs and umbrellas set up. Maybe she should have gone inside for a blanket…

"Hang on a sec," Domenico said, removing his jacket and placing it on the sand.

"Thank you," she said, awkwardness in the air around them. They didn't do nice or gentlemanly. They argued, they teased, they annoyed… Nice was awkward.

Still, she sat on the jacket and tucked her legs to the side as he sat on the sand next to her.

He looked unfazed. Somehow Domenico Kasa—billionaire, former tennis pro playboy—made it seem like sitting on sand in a tuxedo was an everyday occurrence. The tuxedo company should hire him for an ad campaign. The Kasa brothers really did embody the spirit of the island. Part of their success came from the way they integrated into the lifestyle so well. Guests truly felt as though they were staying with family when they visited the resort.

Domenico popped the cork of the champagne with a loud explosion, followed by a stream of liquid spilling down the side of the bottle. He poured a glass for her and handed it to her before filling a glass for himself.

"To a successful first day," he said, clinking his glass to hers.

"One day down, six to go," she said before sipping the champagne. The bubbles danced on her tongue and warmed her. It was the first thing she'd consumed all day besides the taste-testing she'd done in the kitchen during prep. She hadn't even thought about eating an actual meal, but now she kind of wished Domenico had packed a snack for their late-night beach picnic.

"Hungry?" he asked as though reading her mind.

She laughed. "Is it obvious?"

"I can hear your stomach growling," he said, reaching into his pocket.

"Tell me you stuffed galani into your pockets."

Domenico grinned as he shook his head. "I did get the servers to put some away for me, though." He retrieved his cell phone instead and opened an app.

"What are you doing?" she asked, leaning closer to see the Kasa de Paradise guest services app.

"Ordering room service from the twenty-four-hour snack shack," he said, hitting a few items on the list.

Her eyes widened. "To the beach?"

"Yes."

Kasa de Paradise really was a no-wish-went-unserved oasis.

She stared out at the dark ocean waves as he

finished placing the order, then tucked his phone back in his pocket.

Silence lingered in the air around them. But for the first time, it wasn't the awkward, strained, tense silence that often enveloped them. She cast a sideways glance at him. He looked so handsome in the light of the moon breaking through a thin cloud layer overhead and the resort lights in the distance behind them.

"So…why the change of heart on the drink?" she asked.

"No change of heart. I just wanted you to say yes, and when you hesitated, I took offence."

His honesty surprised her. "But yet somehow here we are."

"Because ultimately I go after what I want."

Holy hell. He was hot.

All evening at the masquerade, she'd felt his gaze on her, and she'd had similar trouble focusing on overseeing the food service. The way he'd moved about the room, talking to guests, surveying and observing everything. Anticipated guest needs before they did. His presence strongly felt in the room.

"You did good today," he said, changing the subject as he turned to look at her.

"You're surprised?"

"No. Just annoyed to be proven wrong." That sexy grin of his was back. Only she'd just recently—as in the last twelve hours recently—come to see it as sexy. Before, it was irritating and condescending. Odd how one ill-timed kiss could change things.

Or had it started with that old photo bringing back memories of years of friendship followed by a hurtful drifting apart?

"So you're admitting that you were wrong about me?" She eyed him over the rim of the champagne glass as she took another sip.

"About your abilities as a chef… The rest I'm not sure of."

He meant her character, her intentions…and she wished she could be offended, hand him back his champagne and leave him on the beach alone, but she did have ulterior motives for being there that week and she was gambling with his resort, so she remained silent.

"I'm sure you have some preconceived notions about me too."

She nodded. "I'm not sure how wrong mine are, though."

"Wow. Okay."

"Are you actually able to deny that you are arrogant, moody, self-centered and…"

He held up a hand. "One at a time."

She grinned, feeling a warmth seep across her chest. Must be the champagne. "Okay. Arrogant."

He nodded and took a breath before answering. "It's confidence. Arrogance is talk without action. I put into action every plan I set for myself, and I don't rest until the outcome is the one I expect."

Okay…she could see that rationale. Sort of. He wasn't wrong. He had achieved every goal he'd set for himself. To outside appearances, at least.

"Moody," she said. He couldn't deny that one.

"I prefer brooding—like those men in the Jane Austen era."

She laughed. "That's the vibe you're going for?"

He nodded. "Eighteenth century English nobleman vibes—yeah—the chicks dig it."

"Mr. Darcy you are not, and I'm going to pretend you did not just say *chicks*," she told him, but she couldn't help but smile. This felt…nice. An odd sense of nostalgia was somehow wrapping itself around her—a strange sense of familiarity as though a part of her had never forgotten this connection they'd shared in childhood.

"What else did you call me?"

"Um…" What was the third thing? She thought for a moment. "Self-centered!"

This time he didn't need time to think. "I wouldn't say self-centered. I'd say self-*focused.* I'm consistently striving to be a better version of myself than I was the day before, and I don't allow people to see the work behind that. Therefore they only see the end product, not the struggle, indecision or second-guessing I put myself through. The sacrifices. What I'm giving up—the relationships—I'm giving up to pursue that higher level of fulfillment and awareness."

"Is that why you're a playboy? Too self-*focused* to give attention to a woman."

"Too self-focused to give the *deserved* attention to the *right* woman, yes."

She could hardly criticize that. Wasn't she the same? Hadn't she said countless times that it would take the right man to make her switch her laser focus on building her family business back to what it once was? She was putting herself and her future ahead of all else. "Fair enough."

"And who says I'm a playboy?" he asked with a puzzled look.

Was he serious? "Um…every tabloid…ever."

He scoffed. "I don't read that shit."

Unfortunately, she had! "Maybe not, but the media had a field day with your dating life."

Domenico looked annoyed. "My perceived dating life."

"Oh, those photos looked legit." Did she sound jealous? She hoped not, but truth was, she had been back then. Very much so.

"Those were PR relationships."

She frowned as she looked at him. "What now?"

He sighed. "Publicity driven to help secure attention from the media."

Her eyes widened, and her mouth dropped. "So they weren't real?"

"Nah," Domenico said. "Are you kidding? I was too busy training to actually have a relationship."

Her mind was blown.

All this time thinking he'd been off dating these beautiful athletes with similar drives and passions to his…

This information could have been useful beforc now.

They sipped their champagne and sat silently together. Then Domenico glanced at her. "What about you? Anyone special in your life?"

Adriana shook her head slowly. "I've dated a few men since Leo." *A few* might be an exaggeration. It had bcen two. Barely memorable. "But nothing even close to serious. There was always just something missing. A spark."

Domenico laughed and shook his head.

"What's so funny?"

"Just that I didn't believe in all that spark stuff…" He turned to face her and stared deep into her eyes. "Until you nearly electrocuted me with that kiss."

Their gazes locked, and the heat and passion between them were undeniable. His dark eyes reflected the light coming from the moon as they burned into hers. She glanced at his full lips, and the temptation to lean in and get another taste was overwhelming...but they were getting along and keeping their hands and lips to themselves.

Friends. Colleagues. This was good.

At least, that's what she was telling herself.

Slightly flustered, she looked away. "Anyway, the restaurant takes up most of my time."

"How's it doing?" he asked as he reached for the bottle of champagne and topped up her glass.

Adriana stared into her champagne flute. "Not great. There are always so many new places opening up."

"Bellarini's is part of the culture, the landscape, the tradition."

"Tell that to the tourists."

He nodded. "But surely locals are still loyal."

She sighed. "They are, but most are aging, and since the pandemic, a lot of people order in still—as though they'd forgotten that the best part of eating out was that sense of community, the late nights lingering and talking and drinking... Takeout orders result in half the bill."

"That would have an impact."

She was pensive for a moment. Then, "My brother wants to change the menu. He thinks it's old-fashioned and dated, and he's suggesting including healthier options. Low-carb pasta, almond flour garlic cheese toast."

Domenico shivered. "Disgusting."

"Exactly. Thank you."

Adriana and Domenico shared another look.

This connection, the fact that he got it, got her, surprised her.

Their gazes on one another lingered a dangerously long time. He seemed to be drinking her in, looking straight into her soul. Seeing something…what? Whatever it was, he seemed lost in it, intoxicated by it.

She couldn't remember the last time a man had looked at her like this.

They could be friends and colleagues tomorrow. What would one more kiss hurt? They'd already crossed the line anyway.

Domenico seemed to be thinking the same thing as he moved toward her on the sand. She slid her own body closer, her gaze never breaking contact with his.

His eyes left hers briefly to glance at her lips, and her tongue slid along her bottom one. His expression was full of fiery desire when his eyes met hers again. Her entire body tingled with a longing, an anticipation, a desire to crawl into his arms and kiss him until the sun came up the next morning.

He reached for her and…

Headlights illuminated the beach, headed toward them. The light grew brighter quickly.

Domenico pulled away and jumped to his feet. "That would be our food."

An island cruiser approached with a crew member behind the wheel.

Still slightly dazed, Adriana nodded, fighting the disappointment she felt at the interruption. "The service here is amazing." Too amazing. If only the guy had shown up a bit later…a lot later. Suddenly she wasn't hungry anymore. At least not for food.

Domenico winked at her as he walked backward toward the cruiser. "You have no idea."

Adriana felt a rush of heat flow through her. She didn't doubt his words one little bit. Domenico might not give his time to just any woman, but she suspected when he did give his time and attention to someone, he did it with the same intensity and drive he displayed in the rest of his life.

And suddenly—out of absolutely nowhere—she was desperate to be that one woman.

The food was gone. The champagne was finished. Now what?

Obviously the evening was coming to an end. But he didn't want it to.

Domenico threw their garbage into the trash container on the beach as Adriana dusted the sand off his jacket. She approached and handed it back to him. “Thank you.”

“You’re welcome.”

His gaze locked with hers, and he stared into the depths of her eyes, the moon lighting them up in an intoxicating way. They’d been silent as they’d eaten, but it had been a comfortable, easy silence, not the awkward, tension-filled one they usually endured around one another.

“Guess I should…” she began.

“Want to go for a walk before we call it a night?”

They spoke at the same time, and Domenico nodded. “You’re right, it’s getting late.”

Adriana shook her head. “It’s not that late.”

It was, in fact—just after midnight, and she would have to be back in the kitchen early again the next morning. But he couldn’t seem to let guilt about keeping her out late or the reminder of how important it was for her to do her job right stop him from extending a hand toward her.

Adriana looked at it with a slight expression of surprise, but then slid her hand into his.

Domenico held it tight and kept it in his as they walked along the beach. He glanced toward her, and his breath caught in his chest at the sight of her dark hair blowing in the night breeze. She looked peacefully out at the white caps crashing along the sand in the distance. "You look stunning tonight, by the way."

Adriana's smile was somewhat shy, and she looked caught off guard by the compliment.

"I mean in a non-sexual-harassment kind of way."

She laughed. "Don't worry. I won't report you to HR." She smiled at him, and he swallowed the lump in his throat at the sight.

She was even more beautiful in the moonlight, relaxed and content—with him. That was the most incredible part.

She cleared her throat. "Hey, uh… Leo sent me an old photo today…"

She'd received it too? That meant she'd also probably noticed that lovesick expression he'd had on his face. How did he play this? Admit that he'd seen it too and try to play off the look as nothing…or pretend he had no idea what photo she was talking about?

"Oh yeah…" He wanted to see what she had to say about it first.

"Yeah, it was of the five of us at the beach."

"Those were great times," he said casually.

She turned to look at him. "You remember those summers?"

Only every other memory…since he'd seen that photo again. The sound of her laughter as she'd jumped off the rocks on the cliff into the water below. The way her dark hair always lightened with auburn streaks once the summer sun had gotten to it. The smell of her coconut tanning lotion on her dark skin at the end of the day when she'd hold his waist sitting on the back of his bike as he'd drive them home from the lake. "I mean, vaguely." What was wrong with him?

Her look of mild disappointment had him stopping to turn toward her.

"I remember them very well," he said. "And Leo sent me the photo too."

Adriana nodded. Their gazes met and held for a long breath before they continued walking along the sand.

"Do you visit your mom often?" she asked.

"The last Sunday of every month. We meet for breakfast when I head to the mainland for new tennis inventory."

"How is she? Without your dad?"

"Shc misses him a lot, obviously, but she's doing okay. She has a new wine and book club, and she's teaching a seniors yoga class—staying busy." He paused. "You should stop by to see her. I know she'd love that."

Adriana nodded. "After the breakup, I wasn't sure…"

"She always said you were the daughter she'd hoped Mario would be," he said with a grin.

Adriana turned and swatted at him. "She never said that!"

He laughed. "No, but she always loved you like her own." His mother had always said she was perfectly content to have three boys, but he knew secretly she'd loved having Adriana around. His mother had been hoping Adriana and Leo would get married and grace her with grandbabies.

The thought made Domenico's stomach flip. "Hey, uh…we should probably get you to bed."

She raised an eyebrow as she glanced at him.

"That wasn't an invitation of any sort. No need to alert HR." Not that he wouldn't mind tucking her into bed that night…

She nodded. Hand in hand, they walked along a trail back towards her suite with Domenico leading the way.

Moments later, Domenico and Adriana lingered outside. Adriana toyed with the room key. "I had fun tonight." She laughed. "I mean, not the masquerade party, but after—with you."

"Me too," he said sincerely.

Adriana hesitated, glancing at the key in her hand. "Well…good night."

"'Night."

Adriana sighed as she turned to go inside.

*Say something.*

It had been a special night. He'd had an amazing time with her. Holding her hand, walking, talking—she'd enjoyed it all too. He didn't want it to be the end. He didn't want her to go to bed that night without plans to spend time together again.

Despite common sense, he wanted to spend time with her this week on the island.

Did she want that too?

"Hey…" he said, a thought suddenly plaguing him.

"Yeah?" She turned back quickly as though relieved there was more than just a good-night.

"Did you really think I was off jet-setting the world with different female athletes?"

Adriana sighed and nodded. "Your PR person did their job well." She paused, and then her gaze met his. "Well enough that I didn't see any reason not to date your brother."

The realization hit him straight in the chest. Adriana had believed he was dating other people—despite his heartfelt letters and the fact that he'd only ever thought about her when he was away. A deep regret filled him that he'd never even thought about the effect his public persona would have on her.

She turned back toward the building in his moment of silent contemplation. "'Night, Dom."

"Hey…" He couldn't end the night like this, but he wasn't sure what exactly to say.

She turned back…again. "Yeah?"

"I have an opening for an early tennis lesson tomorrow morning…if you're interested." Not exactly smooth, but it was all he could think of in the moment that didn't sound completely desperate. He was offering her a tennis lesson. Made sense, and it was at least a way to gauge if she wanted to spend time with him again.

Adriana sent him a teasing grin. "You sure Mrs. Conway won't be jealous?"

If she caught them, she absolutely would. But it was probably the last reason why it wasn't a good idea. He was choosing not to entertain the other reasons.

"Is that a yes?"

Adriana shrugged casually, but he could tell she was just as happy to have an excuse to spend time with him as he was with her, which had his heart pounding and a warmth flowing through him at the anticipation of it that he hadn't experienced around a woman in a very long time.

"Why not?" she said. "I mean, how often does one get an opportunity to be taught by a tennis pro, right?"

"Great! See you at tennis court B at four thirty," Domenico said as he headed toward the island cruiser.

"Four thirty a.m.? What? No, that's like three hours from now," Adriana said.

Domenico grinned as he jumped onto the cruiser. "Better get some sleep, then." He winked and waved as he started the cruiser.

It kicked up a cloud of sand as he tore away from the building, feeling exhilarated. He wouldn't be getting any sleep that evening.

# CHAPTER SEVEN

A GENTLE BREEZE blew through the open patio door as the early morning sun rose over the island in the distance. Wide awake, Adriana sat in her bed, coffee cup in one hand, her cell phone in the other—the contact list open to Domenico's name.

She should cancel.

She kept staring at the message thread where the last text from him had been Yep. Confirming his attendance to a surprise birthday dinner for Leo four years ago. She expected to see typing dots appear any second when he too came to the realization that this was not a good idea.

The night before had been magical.

Surreal.

But in the light of day, they couldn't keep spending time together like that. Holding hands? What had they been thinking? Those long, intense, gazes—holy hell! They were asking for trouble.

How had they even gotten to this point?

She mentally recapped the last forty-eight hours.

Arriving on the pier to meet grumpy Dom.

Bickering in the kitchen.

Mild irritation—turned to attraction with the late-night snack incident—aka abs.

Full-on heated exchange in the kitchen that led to the most passionate kiss of her life.

Then, a successful event followed by the most incredible evening with the mind-blowing realization that all those years thinking he was living this playboy lifestyle had been a falsified narrative for promotion?

She wasn't even sure what to do with that information as she stared at the message thread. Domenico may not have been the playboy the media had made him out to be—made her believe him to be—but he'd still developed a massive ego and acted as though she didn't exist for all those years. That had hurt too…

She had to cancel.

This early-morning tennis lesson had nothing to do with tennis, and they both knew it. He'd panicked, wanting to spend more time with her but not knowing how to ask, and she'd agreed for the same reason.

But it had to have been just the island's beauty, the salty air and glow of the moonlight combined with the champagne, that had made them both get swept away in the moment.

That morning, he too had to be realizing this wasn't a good idea.

Typing dots!

Adriana sat straighter abruptly, nearly spilling her coffee.

She waited…

No message. No more typing dots.

Seriously Dom?

What had he been about to say?

She bit her lip. Should she text him?

No, then he'd know she'd been sitting there staring at his name on her phone.

She sighed and waited, but when no more typing dots appeared and the time on her phone revealed four fifteen, she swung her legs over the side of the bed and got up.

She went to the dresser where housekeeping had unpacked her clothing for her with turndown service the night before and opened a drawer. She didn't really have tennis appropriate gear. Just shorts and sports bras for working out, if she had the time.

She reached in and selected a cute pale pink set—tight shorts, bra top and matching half sweater that she'd bought for a yoga class where the instructor had been hot, but he'd only been teaching as a fill-in so he'd never gotten to see her in it.

She got dressed and stared at her reflection in the mirror. She looked sporty sexy. Was that the vibe she wanted to go with?

*OMG Adriana! It's just a workout outfit! Quit overthinking it!* What else was she supposed to wear working out?

Okay, she could have gone with a frumpy T-shirt…

She was reading way too much into the clothing choice.

Domenico saw women dressed in skimpy tennis outfits all the time. Her outfit probably wouldn't even register on his radar.

Dressed in his tennis gear, Domenico waited on tennis court B for Adriana. He checked his watch and ran a hand through his hair. "What am I doing?" he muttered. This was not a good idea. Why had he suggested it the night before? The chemistry between them had been off the charts, and she'd practically been begging for a good-night kiss—the lingering outside the room door, the fidgeting with the keys, the teasing. Adriana didn't linger, fidget or tease! At least not with him!

This was bad. Very, very bad.

He couldn't be entertaining these feelings with his brother's ex-girlfriend.

Though last night's revelation that she'd agreed to date Leo because she thought he'd been seeing other people had him spiraling. He couldn't believe all this time, he'd been hurt by a betrayal that he'd essentially caused.

Still, he should cancel this lesson before things got complicated.

He'd tried. He'd opened his phone to their message thread. Typed…deleted. Typed and deleted.

But the truth was, he wanted to see her again this morning. And whether it was nostalgia from that old photo or the heat from the kiss in the kitchen or the romantic island vibes the night before as they'd walked hand in hand along the sand in the moonlight, all he knew was that he'd wanted to see her again.

They'd once been friends, and maybe a part of him just wanted that back—the friendship.

Adriana rounded the corner on the trail headed toward the court, and Domenico saw her approach.

It was so much more than wanting his buddy back.

His gaze swept over her—took in the tight pink curve-hugging yoga shorts, the bra top that barely contained her amazing breasts and the light sweater that hung casually off one shoulder. One beautiful, perfect shoulder with tiny little freckles that he just wanted to connect with his tongue.

So very badly.

"Sorry I'm late," Adriana said, stopping in front of him.

"I'm actually surprised you showed up at all." Honest caution. Obviously, his nervous system believed it was the best way to approach this situation they found themselves in.

Adriana nodded and released a breath as though she had been spiraling with this all morning. "Me too." She hesitated. "Do you think this is a good idea?"

"Teaching you to play tennis? If I remember correctly, you suck at it, so it can't hurt." Jokes. His nerves had moved on to jokes.

Adriana shot him a look. "You know what I mean. What are we doing, Dom?"

How did he know?

Domenico sighed. "Leo told me to play nice, so that's what I'm doing." *Okay, we're lying now.*

"And that's it?"

Was she relieved? Disappointed? Not buying his BS?

He studied her, but her expression was neutral—giving absolutely nothing away. She had to know that wasn't it. The kiss should have told her it was far more than that. The hand-holding on the beach and the long, intense gazes filled with so many unspoken words…hell, that old photo…

Domenico nodded. "That's it." Panic.

"Okay…" Adriana removed the tiny half-sweater thing and placed her hands on her hips as she scanned the courts. "Where do we start?"

*By putting that sweater back on.* How was he supposed to concentrate on teaching her anything when she was standing there looking like… that? Curves for days, her ample breasts filling out the strappy sports bra, her tight stomach—all on display. The sight of her would throw the best tennis player completely off their game, and he didn't claim to be the best anymore.

With her looking like that, he'd barely be an adequate instructor.

And he wasn't buying that innocent look on her face—not even for a second. She had to know how amazingly hot she looked in that outfit. Those sports store manufacturers shouldn't be allowed to sell sexy workout clothes. They were a major distraction.

But if Adriana knew the effect she was having on him, she was hiding it as she stood there looking at him expectantly. "Well? Let's go, tennis pro."

Right. Teach her how to play tennis.

And try not to get too turned on in the meantime.

Domenico looked away as he took a deep breath. "Okay, let's get you a racket." He approached his gear, selected one for her and extended it.

Adriana took it and of course held it wrong.

Domenico sighed. "Like this," he said. Standing behind her and wrapping his arms around her, he positioned her hands on the racket. "This hand here...this hand here."

His breath was blowing the tendrils of hair that had escaped her ponytail at the nape of her neck, and he could see tiny goose bumps surface on her skin. It was twenty-seven degrees outside already this morning. She certainly wasn't cold.

"Okay, let's try serving the ball," he said, taking a ball out of his pocket. His hands still around her, he tossed the ball up in the air and helped her swing at it. They missed.

"Let's try again," he said, taking another ball from his pocket. He moved in closer to her, his full body connecting to hers. His hands around hers, their grips tight on the racket. He breathed in the sweet scent of her and took in the new view of her cleavage from this vantage point. Could she feel how turned on he was?

The temptation to toss the tennis racket aside, turn her around to face him and kiss her until they were both hot and sweaty for other reasons was overwhelming.

She turned her head to look up at him. “You good?”

Oh, he was great. Just desiring a woman he shouldn’t have been.

“Yeah,” he said, tossing the ball into the air. They swung, and the racket connected with it. The ball sailed effortlessly over the net to the other, empty side of the court. “Not bad.” He slowly released her, despite every inch of him wanting to hold on. “Think you can do that? On your own?” Standing there any longer with his arms around her would only lead to trouble.

A lot of trouble.

She swallowed hard and nodded. “Yeah, I think I got it.”

“Great.” Twirling his racket in his hand—a long-time nervous energy habit of his—he made his way to the other side of the court, and that’s when he noticed…

Pricilla watching them from the balcony of her villa. Even from that distance, he could tell she didn’t look happy.

“You know how to play tennis—you taught me,” her best friend Isabella said through the cell phone screen later that morning.

Grabbing a set of oven mitts, Adriana opened

the oven door and took out a veggie lasagna, then popped a meat one in before answering. "I know, but he offered, and I…"

"Wanted to stroke his ego?"

Wanted to stroke the muscular forearms wrapped around her, mostly. She shook her head as she approached a mixing bowl and poured flour into it. "I'm just trying to keep the peace—for the sake of the review."

"Your plan was to steer clear of him."

"Well, he's making that difficult, observing my every move." And eyeing her like he wanted to eat her for breakfast. The way he'd looked at her in her workout gear this morning had confirmed that hot yoga instructor totally would have asked her out had he seen her in it.

Too bad.

"Isn't that annoying though?"

"It was at first. But I understand he just wants to make sure everything goes well. There's a lot at stake."

Isabella eyed her. "Oh my God. You're falling for him."

Adriana reached for the salt to add to the bowl. "Nope. No. Not even a little. That's ridiculous." She poured the salt in and started to stir.

Isabella raised an eyebrow in amusement. "Then why did you just add sugar instead of salt to that bread?"

Adriana's eyes widened as she glanced at the container. She sighed and shot Isabella a look. "Cause you're distracting me."

"Uh-huh… I'm not the one distracting you." Isabella looked seriously unimpressed.

"What can I say? I don't know why, but all of a sudden, there's…an attraction there." She lowered her voice.

"It's Leo's brother."

"I know!"

"And technically your boss."

"I know! I know." She'd been telling herself the same things over and over. Unfortunately, once she was around Domenico again, common sense went out the window.

"Stay focused. Keep your head in the game," Isabella said.

"I will," she said, dumping the contents of the bowl and starting over.

"It smells delicious in here." Linda entered, sniffing the aroma.

"Gotta go," Adriana told Isabella, disconnecting the FaceTime call and smiling to greet the reviewer. "Good morning, Ms. Frank. How was your breakfast?"

The reviewer was dressed in her usual neutral colors that day with seafoam-green jewelry accents that Adriana recognized as items from the gift shop—a good sign.

"Compliments to the chef. I've never had crispy salt-and-pepper French toast before. I admit I was skeptical, but you made me a believer."

Adriana's smile widened as she nodded. "As kids, my brother hated how maple syrup makes French toast soggy—it's a texture thing. My grandmother came up with the recipe for him. It's definitely a favorite at Bellarini's."

Linda leaned against the counter and nodded. "Your family's restaurant in Naples, right? I remember seeing it from my research of the staff."

The woman was thorough—it didn't surprise her that she knew everything about each of the staff at Kasa de Paradise. In her online search, she'd probably also discovered the previous relationship between Adriana and Leo. There were plenty of photos of the two of them together online with the announcement and grand opening of the resort. Should she address it?

"Yes. I'm only here for the week," she said.

"Ah..." Linda made a note on her clipboard.

Uh-oh, maybe she shouldn't have said that. "But I also helped design this kitchen before the resort opened. Would you like a more complete tour?" she added quickly.

Linda nodded, then said, "Do you happen to have any more of that French toast hidden in here?"

Adriana laughed. "Absolutely." She opened the fridge and retrieved the container of leftover French toast. She opened the lid and handed Linda another slice.

Linda carried it and ate as Adriana toured her around the kitchen.

"When Leo and I first talked about the kitchen design, we were immediately on the same page. We wanted to prioritize functionality and efficiency, featuring professional-grade appliances, ample workspace, and tools to facilitate culinary endeavors, with an emphasis on workflow and ease of movement for multiple cooks."

Linda nodded her approval as she chewed. "I suspect it's a pleasure to cook here, but nothing beats the intimacy of a crammed, busy, chaotic kitchen—like the one I'm sure you have at Bellarini's."

Adriana laughed at the accuracy. "Bellarini's kitchen is a closet compared to this one, and while it has professional appliances, they don't compare to the quality at Kasa de Paradise. But somehow the closeness and chaotic nature seem to add flavor and a sense of home-cooked charm to the meals. As if the food absorbs the love and commitment the kitchen staff have for one another and the pride we put into every dish."

Linda stared at her as she spoke, and Adriana realized she'd taken the focus off this kitchen.

"But this kitchen is superb!" she said quickly, gesturing to the appliances. "Professional-grade ovens, a powerful gas range with high BTU burners, and a robust ventilation system to handle intense heat and smoke. Warming drawers to keep food hot and multiple ovens, including convection and steam models." They continued to walk through the area, and Adriana pointed out the other amazing features. "Expansive marble countertops and large islands that provide additional prep space and often serve as a central hub for staff to work together. Multiple deep sinks with high-arc faucets, pot fillers over the range, and large, well-organized pantry storage. Sub-Zero refrigerators and freezers are amazing for their capacity and freshness-preserving features."

Linda nodded and took notes as they continued the tour.

Adriana glanced at the notepad—all positive comments so far. She breathed a sigh of relief as she summed it all up. "The overall design emphasizes workflow and efficiency, with appliances and tools strategically placed for easy access and seamless transitions between tasks."

Linda popped the last of her French toast into her mouth and made a final note. "Thank you for that tour—very thorough." She closed her eyes as she chewed. When she swallowed the bite, she opened them. "But now for the most important question."

Adriana held her breath. *Don't mess this up.*

"You make this French toast at your restaurant, Bellarini's? It's a menu staple?"

Adriana relaxed as she nodded with a proud smile. "Every Sunday for brunch."

Linda licked her fingers. "Then expect me for brunch whenever I'm on this side of the world."

Adriana beamed. "Thank you. We'd love to host you—as my guest."

"You truly are a talented chef—Adriana. My sampling tray was incredible. I assume you learned to cook from your family?"

She nodded. "My father and grandmother taught me. My mother was an amazing chef as well, but she passed away when I was little. My grandmother taught me all the family recipes, and then my father taught me how to make them on a larger scale—a little faster and cost-effectively without losing the quality and taste we've been known for for generations."

Adriana's smile faded at the sound of a throat clearing in the kitchen doorway. She turned to see Domenico standing there—an unreadable expression on his face.

Had he heard her go on about Bellarini's?

He looked amazing—showered and now

dressed in khaki shorts and a navy button-down collared shirt, open at the throat.

The temptation to slide her hands inside that open collar…

"Ready for the Jet Ski tour, Ms. Frank?" he said, interrupting Adriana's thoughts.

"Yes!" Linda said excitedly. She turned back to Adriana. "Thank you again. Quite impressive."

Adriana nodded politely, her gaze sliding to Domenico.

His proud and grateful look made her breath catch in her chest.

"Shall we?" he said to Linda, extending an elbow to guide her out of the kitchen.

The reviewer took one look at the exposed forearms below the rolled shirtsleeves and eagerly linked her hand through. "We shall."

Lucky woman.

I need to see you in the office.

That's all the text message said, but Domenico's heart pounded in his ears as he made his way to the office, still dressed in his wetsuit from the Jet Ski tour with Linda Frank—one that would have been a lot of fun had he not been stressing out over Leo's text message the whole time.

Did he know about his and Adriana's late-night rendezvous? Or the early-morning tennis lesson? Had Pricilla said something? Complained about his rudeness the night before or embellished what she'd witnessed between him and Adriana on the tennis court that morning?

Sweat gathered on his lower back under the unforgiving wetsuit material as he entered the office.

Leo finished a call and hung up the phone, then glanced up at him. His expression was unreadable. Then he laughed. "You could have changed first."

"Thought it might be urgent," he said awkwardly, but relaxing slightly. If his brother was upset, he wouldn't be laughing at Domenico's appearance.

"You're dripping all over the floor," Leo said, smile gone, a slight annoyance taking its place.

Domenico sighed. "What did you want?"

"I have to head over to the mainland tonight. There's a problem with the new linens we ordered for the guest villas. They got the sizing wrong, and..."

Leo kept talking, but all Domenico heard was that his brother would be off the island that evening.

Domenico shoved his hands in his pockets and nodded, desperately trying to hide how excited he was at the news. Guilty too, but mostly excited. There was no point denying he wanted to spend more time alone with Adriana, exploring the connection from last night and this morning. And hearing her talk about the kitchen at Bellarini's and hearing her passion for her career and her family restaurant this morning had made him melt a little. Sure, she'd been supposed to talking up the state-of-the-art kitchen at Kasa de Paradise, but he couldn't fault her pride in her family's business and the generations of chefs that had taught her everything she knew. It was endearing.

So, why was he struggling to quiet the nagging thought in the back of his mind that she might still have an ulterior motive for being here. Probably because she did—securing a good review of the food on Kasa Island would help her family restaurant—but was that really so wrong? Win-win… Unless she jeopardized what guests expected from their resort in favor of making food that would get Linda Frank to write highly of her culinary skills. Linda's review was important, but the experience of guests was still first and foremost.

"No problem. I can hold down the fort," he said casually.

Leo eyed him suspiciously. "What's up with you?"

"Nothing." Too quick. Too high-pitched.

*Calm down, Dom. She might not even want to see you tonight.*

Though the expression on her face in the kitchen earlier that day said otherwise.

Leo continued to study him intently. Sweat collected on Domenico's forehead and dripped into his eyes under his brother's scrutiny. The Kasa brothers were close. Too close. And Domenico was the one with the worst poker face. He could never successfully hide anything from them. As kids, when they got in trouble, he always got them grounded with his inability to lie or pull a fast one on their parents.

"You seem different," Leo said.

"I'm not different."

Leo nodded emphatically. "You totally are. You're less…on edge. Like, if I didn't know better, I'd think you'd gotten laid for a change."

He wished. His pulse raced, and his mouth went dry. He may not have gotten laid the night before, but Leo's spidey senses weren't completely off the mark. He had to be careful. Maybe he should tell him…but that was a discussion he had to have with Adriana first. Confessing to Leo had to be a joint decision. One they were both on board for and ready for the consequences of. "I assure you I'm still as focused as ever."

Leo laughed, and Domenico's shoulders relaxed.

Interrogation over.

"Okay, well, I'm going to go get changed." He turned and headed toward the door.

"Hey." His brother's voice made him pause. "Late-night craving last night?" Leo asked behind him.

Domenico swung around to see his brother reviewing an invoice on the desk.

New panic gripped his chest. "What do you mean?" he asked slowly.

"Last night. There was a midnight food delivery on the resort app with your signature."

Right. His brothers had access to the app just as well as he did. Wow, he really wasn't good at sneaking around. Which was why he shouldn't be. And if he and Adriana were going to keep… hanging out, they'd need to be honest. Soon. Just not right this second.

"Oh, yeah… Didn't eat much at the event. Nervous stomach."

"Looks like a lot of food for one person." Leo eyed him. "Do I need to remind you of the policy you created? No dating guests?"

Domenico shook his head so fast, his neck cramped. "That's not happening. I was just hungry. Really hungry."

Leo shot him a chastising look. "Adriana's

not going to poison you with her food. At least, I don't think so."

Domenico cleared his throat. "About Adriana..."

Leo glanced up at him expectantly.

*I like her. I'm insanely attracted to her.*

Nope. He couldn't out them without her permission.

"She's turning out to be a great help."

Leo nodded as he stood and gathered his things. "Speaking of..." Leo picked up a stack of résumés and handed them to Domenico as he exited the office. "Find us a new head chef. Adriana's made it clear she's a limited-time offer."

And one that shouldn't be on offer to him.

# CHAPTER EIGHT

A TENNIS BALL sailed over the net and was returned with impressive speed and precision, catching Domenico so off guard, he almost missed returning the shot.

*What the?*

That afternoon, Pricilla was unusually focused for her lesson and not her usual flirty self.

Domenico struggled for breath as he tried to keep up with her unexpected pace. He returned the ball a little harder and faster, and she expertly returned it. He hurried to the opposite side of the court, but he wasn't quick enough.

Match point for Pricilla.

*Since when?* He slaughtered her most days. He nodded, impressed, as he approached the net. "Wow. You've gotten a lot better," he said knowingly. He could recognize when he'd been played.

"I might not have been completely honest about my skill level," Pricilla said coyly. That day she was dressed more the part with a tennis outfit that covered most of her assets but was still flattering.

Trying a new tactic to get his attention, perhaps?

"Hustling me?" he teased, keeping the mood light. She'd been cool and distant when they'd arrived and clearly still annoyed from the night before's brush-off at the masquerade event, but he hoped this meant she'd gotten the hint. Maybe she'd stop coming on to him.

Instead, Pricilla leaned over the net, giving him ample view of her cleavage. "I think we both know why I requested these lessons," she said in a tone only describable as a fierce feline in heat.

Domenico shifted uncomfortably. So much for retreating. She looked even more determined and on her game now. He almost preferred the flirty, flighty Pricilla. He'd welcome that version back over this driven-to-get-what-she-wanted alpha female standing across from him.

How did he let this woman down gently? Refuse her advances *again* without upsetting her? A high-class guest with friends all over Europe was not the enemy he wanted to have or one the resort could afford. A one-star Yelp review from Pricilla Conway would outweigh a million five-stars. Not to mention a disgruntled guest while Linda was still here was not ideal.

He cleared his throat. "Mrs. Conway…you are

an amazing woman, but we have a policy not to get…" he paused and lowered his voice as another couple arrived on the courts and waved at them "…intimately involved with our guests."

Couldn't argue with corporate policy, right?

Pricilla moved closer, grabbed the front of his sweaty shirt, pulled him in and whispered in his ear, "I won't tell."

Domenico guessed influential, powerful seductresses didn't care about corporate policy. Or causing a mild scene in front of the other resort guests.

Aware of the other couple's intrigued expressions and their eyes on them, Domenico reached for her hand and gently untangled her fingers from the fabric of his shirt, then moved away. "You're here with your husband," he said gently. She had to respect him for not wanting to put her in a compromising position in her marriage.

Pricilla's demeanor turned frosty, and her expression was one that would reduce a boardroom full of executives to a weeping puddle of dress shoes and ties. "Do you have a point?" she said in a clipped tone.

Obviously not.

Domenico sighed. "I'm sorry… I didn't mean to offend or to imply…"

"Does the resort also have a policy about owners getting intimately involved with hired staff?" Her voice was a little too high.

Domenico stilled as he glanced quickly at the other couple, who weren't even trying to hide their interest in their conversation. "It does," he said quietly through clenched teeth.

"You have no problem bending one rule but not another?"

"I don't know what you mean."

Pricilla eyed him, long and penetrating, then she shrugged—the frostiness melting away as though she'd been placed in an oven. "Must be my mistake, then," Pricilla said airily, unfazed as she collected her things and left the court.

Which left him slightly fazed.

What was he doing pacing outside the main building, waiting for Adriana to finish up for the evening? He should go to his villa for the rest of the night and quit playing with fire. Especially after his interaction with Pricilla.

Adriana was off-limits.

Sure, they had a connection. Sure, there was more passion in their kiss than he'd felt in ten relationships. And sure, the sexual tension radiating between them that morning had been fire, but...she was still Leo's ex.

And staff.

He was breaking two rules. So far, he'd been

caught breaking one by the feisty, vengeful Pricilla Conway. Which could end up being disastrous enough. He didn't need Leo finding out he'd broken the second one. Otherwise he'd be cleaning up the mess of bad press for the resort and a bloody broken nose.

He should just go. Avoid Adriana as much as possible for the rest of the week, then go back to barely talking for the rest of their lives.

Easy. Done.

Adriana exited the main building, and instead, Domenico approached—his feet on autopilot. "Hey."

Awkward.

"Hey," Adriana said just as awkwardly.

It made him feel a bit better that they both seemed to be alternating between flirting shamelessly obviously and not being able to put a full sentence together.

He cleared his throat. "Dinner service went well."

A neutral compliment. Safe. Couldn't read anything into that.

"I think so..." she said, shuffling her feet and glancing around them.

What now?

The silence grew deafening as a long moment passed with neither of them speaking.

*Just say something, moron!*

She looked amazing in a pale blue tank and cutoffs—not exactly an executive-staff-appropriate off-duty wardrobe, but he had zero issue with her breaking the rules. Lots of rules. All the rules.

Domenico cleared his throat. "I was wondering if maybe you'd like to take a walk?"

Adriana looked conflicted, and he immediately wished he had let her speak first. "I don't know, Dom. Leo isn't going to be okay with this."

So that was her concern too. It made him feel better that Leo was the stumbling block for her and also frustrated. He shouldn't even be putting her in this position. Brothers couldn't date the same woman—full stop. This moral dilemma should have been his cross to bear alone—in secret—the way he'd apparently been carrying it for years.

There was no doubt in his mind that the disdain he'd always felt for Adriana had been repressed attraction and admiration because she was dating his brother. A self-preservation thing.

Why couldn't those feelings have stayed repressed?

Maybe because the situation had changed when he realized that he might have inadvertently driven Adriana into Leo's arms! And now he was constantly spiraling with thoughts of what if.

Either way, Adriana was right, and she was voicing it, so he should respect her internal conflict and acknowledge that she was correct. They should go their separate ways. Put an end to this before it got even more complicated and out of hand.

"Leo's on the mainland tonight," he blurted out instead.

Adriana looked torn but definitely tempted when her gaze met his.

Why was he pressuring her into this when they both knew it was the wrong thing to do? Seriously, what was wrong with him? Was he trying to sabotage everything the brothers had worked hard to achieve together? This would be an act of betrayal that they might not be able to move past.

*Retreat and retract the offer.*

*Tell her she's right—we should forget what happened and not let anything further transpire.*

"Only if you want to," were instead the words that came out of his mouth.

Not exactly retreating and retracting!

Adriana was silent for a torturously long time. Then she said, "I want to."

Oh, thank God.

Only not.

Now that she'd agreed, it felt like they'd taken an unspoken step forward together into deceit and betrayal, which made him uneasy. All those years feeling like Adriana had betrayed him and their friendship in pursuing a relationship with Leo and here he was encouraging actual betrayal…but unfortunately, in that moment, looking into her captivating eyes, all he could think about was the way they'd shone in the moonlight the night before and how her laughter had carried on the breeze and how after leaving her, he'd felt happier, lighter, and more fulfilled than he had in years.

"I'll meet you on the beach in an hour—at sunset?"

She nodded. "At sunset."

The twilight hour known to inspire all kinds of sins.

What was she thinking, pacing the sand, waiting for Domenico to go on another romantic moonlit walk with her?

She was asking for trouble. *They* were asking for trouble. Yet when he'd invited her, her heart had soared, and she'd felt a stirring in her like never before. All day she'd thought of him as she'd worked. While she knew this wasn't a good idea, it was all she longed to do.

As she watched him approach, her palms started to sweat.

Still dressed in the khakis and blue dress shirt from that morning, with his hair slightly windblown, he looked gorgeous. She knew he was just as freaked out and guilty about these growing feelings of attraction as she was, but he too seemed to be pushing them aside in favor of following his own desires.

To be with her.

The thought made her pulse race.

"You showed up," he said as though he'd doubted it.

"So did you."

He nodded and extended a hand to her.

She stared at it for a long moment before sliding hers into it. He held tight as they started to walk along the quiet section of guest-free beach.

"Sorry about this morning—the question tour," she clarified when he looked confused. "I was trying to keep the focus on the resort, but Linda kept bringing her questions back to Bellarini's."

Domenico shook his head. "It was totally fine. Listening to you talk about the family restaurant was really nice. I think it went a long way with her. Your passion as well as your skill." He turned to look at her, and her breath caught in her throat.

The temptation to wrap her arms around his neck and kiss him was insanely strong. But she refused to make that first move. If he wanted to kiss her, he would.

He cleared his throat, and his expression was suddenly serious. "There is one thing we need to be careful of."

"Besides Leo?"

He nodded. "Pricilla Conway."

"Ah, that cougar closet tennis star who's been trying to seduce you."

Domenico's eyes widened. "You knew she was faking it?"

Adriana laughed at his naivety. "You're adorable when you're oblivious."

Domenico shot her a look. "She saw us on the court together this morning."

She nodded, conflict resurfacing. "Maybe we shouldn't be doing this. There's a lot at stake."

Domenico stopped and turned to face her. He reached out and touched her cheek softly. "Believe me, I know. If there was any way I could fight this urge to be with you, I would."

She swallowed hard. His gaze burned into hers and his gentle caress became more of a grip on her as his hand slid to the back of her neck, drawing her closer. She took a step toward him and wrapped her arms around his neck. He peered down at her before slowly lowering his face toward hers.

The kiss was soft, gentle and quick, but it had her entire body on fire.

He pulled back and released a deep breath. "Look, maybe this can't actually go anywhere, but I feel like we should explore this insane and inconvenient attraction—to get it out of our system?"

Adriana nodded. "A short-term fling?"

"Exactly," Dom said. He extended a hand, and Adriana stared at it a beat before accepting it.

They shook. Then quietly, hand in hand, they continued along the beach, a comfortable silence and unspoken understanding between them.

A little while later, a small villa appeared in the distance, and Domenico led the way toward it. "Mi casa," he said.

Adriana looked with admiration at the villa in its simplicity, surrounded by nature. "This is where you live?"

Domenico nodded. "Leo and Mario prefer guest suites in the main building, but I like it out here."

"I can see why. I think you have the best view on the island." Adriana scanned the long, deserted stretch of white sand, the swaying trees and the view of the mainland in the distance, illuminated at night.

Domenico stared at her. He moved closer and touched her cheek. Adriana lifted her chin upwards to stare into his eyes.

"I do right now."

Adriana swallowed hard. "Domenico, I'm enjoying my time with you…"

Domenico caressed the side of her cheek affectionately, moving even closer to her. "But…"

"Leo."

"Yeah. That's a problem, isn't it?" he asked, only moving even closer. He wrapped one arm around her waist and drew her into him.

Adriana didn't resist. "I mean, it is, right? For you too?"

"Of course it is. But I've gotten good at pushing it aside the more time we spend together." Domenico held her tight against him and traced his finger along her jawline.

"We can't do anything to hurt him," Adriana said softly, but the hint of wanting in her tone encouraged him to continue his motions.

"What if he doesn't know?"

"Dom…"

"Look, I love my brother, but things have been over between you two for a long time," he said huskily, rationalizing things for the both of them. He was trying to make them both feel less guilty about their growing, undeniable connection. So far it was working.

Adriana nodded. "Keep talking."

"And Leo loves us both. He'd want us to be happy, right?"

She sighed and cocked her head to the side. "Now you're stretching a little..."

Domenico chuckled softly as he pulled her in even closer, lowered his face toward hers. "Is it working, though? Do you feel at least a little bit better?"

She felt amazing there in his arms, his breath warm against her skin, his lips just inches from hers and his attraction-filled gaze locked on hers. "Yes." The word was no more than a breathy whisper if it existed at all.

Domenico lowered his head further, and his lips met hers. A soft sigh escaped her as Adriana sank into him, giving in to the kiss. Her hands reached up and tangled into the back of his hair, holding his head firmly in place.

He wasn't getting away so quickly this time. She needed this kiss. Longed for it.

His mouth searched hers with a desperation as though he'd never quite be satisfied. She returned the kiss with all the passion in her soul as she clung to him and his arms held her tight.

Both out of breath moments later, they slowly pulled away.

Domenico's gaze was intense, full of attraction as he stared down into her eyes. "Want to come inside?" he asked, his tone gruff.

Adriana didn't hesitate. "More than anything."

Domenico and Adriana entered the villa, kissing and removing one another's clothing as they made their way toward Domenico's bedroom.

Domenico stopped, hesitated as he studied her intently. "You sure about this?"

"About being with you—right here, right now—yes."

Domenico bent at the knees, scooped her up into his arms, carried her inside the room and placed her onto the bed. She scanned the space quickly, taking in the wicker rattan furniture of the room—the four-poster bed and reading chair in the corner—simple island vibes. A curtain blew in the window, and she could hear the waves crashing against the shore outside.

He unbuttoned his shirt and tossed it onto the chair before joining her on the bed.

His body never ceased to impress her. Muscular and sculpted, but also strong and capable—there was a difference. Muscles could be built in a gym but true strength came from years of dedication, hard work, putting his body to the extreme in pursuit of excellence.

Domenico Kasa demanded excellence.

Which made her suddenly very self-conscious

as he reached for her and started to remove her shirt.

"Wait," she said. He instantly stopped, let go of the fabric.

"Sorry."

"No. Don't be sorry. I—uh—I just—um." Rarely was she ever at a loss for words, but how did she tell him that she was nervous he'd see her flaws when he clearly didn't have one, despite her ribbing? "Um..."

"This is a bad idea? You're not comfortable?" he asked, genuinely, sincerely concerned, which just made her want him even more than the sight of the muscles bulging in his biceps.

"Not in the way you mean," she said slowly.

"Okay..."

She sighed. "Look, it's been a while, and I work long hours. I'm not a gym rat, and I love pasta...all kinds of pastas and desserts..."

He frowned quizzically. "I really don't know what you're trying to say."

"I'm not..." She still struggled for the right words. She gestured his physique. "This."

Domenico looked confused for a second. Then he smiled. "I would hope not. If you were, you wouldn't be in my bedroom right now, turning me on, hotter than I've been in years."

She was doing that to him? She knew he was turned on. That was evident by the bulge in the front of his pants. But was he really feeling her as much as she was aching for him?

He touched her cheek gently. "Adriana, since we were kids, I've always thought you were the most breathtaking pain in the ass I'd ever seen."

She'd take it.

She reached for him and pulled him down on top of her. Her mouth crushed his, and he drew back briefly in surprise. "So, we're doing this?"

"Less talk, more getting naked," she said, sitting up and lifting her arms above her head for him to remove her shirt. He did. Then he continued to remove the bra and her shorts, tossing everything aside.

Exposed in only her thong underwear, under his lust-filled gaze, she shivered on the bed.

"Cold?" he asked with a grin, knowing that the shiver was caused by her every nerve ending quivering at the anticipation of his touch, his hands on her flesh, his lips against her skin. "You won't be soon." He spread her legs and lowered himself between them. His hands trailed over her exposed skin at her neck, her chest, between her breasts. His gaze drank her in, following the path of his fingers along her skin.

Adriana's entire body sprang to life beneath his delicate but deliberate touch as his fingers trailed along her stomach…and farther down.

He slipped his hand beneath the lace waistband of her thong as he lowered his head to her nipple, circling it with his tongue before taking it in his mouth and sucking gently. His fingers brushed over a soft mound of bare flesh, reaching her sweet wetness between her legs.

"Dom," she said, arching her back on the bed beneath him.

"Do you like that?"

She nodded, biting her lip to stop from moaning.

His lifted his gaze from her breasts to her face, and he watched her expression as his fingers stroked her.

"You have too many clothes on," she said, desperate to have him as naked as she was. Feel his skin pressed against hers.

He slowly broke away, stood and tore off his khakis…then his briefs.

Adriana took him in, and her heart raced. Domenico Kasa was definitely…proportional. He reached for the waistband of his briefs as he nodded at her thong. "Take that off."

The commanding tone in his voice normally would have irritated her, but in that moment, in that context, she was more than happy to obey.

She slipped her fingers inside the fabric at her hips and slowly shimmied them down over her hips, thighs, legs and feet, tossing the fabric onto the pile of discarded clothing on the floor.

Domenico removed his briefs and stared at her on the bed—naked, waiting, and more than ready for him. “Open for me,” he said. She eagerly complied, spreading her legs apart to allow him to lie between them. The moment his body made contact with hers, he closed his eyes and groaned.

It felt so good. Too good. Dangerously good. She couldn’t wait a second longer.

“Condoms?”

Seconds later, covered, he hesitated, his body aligned with hers, his hands on her waist, ready to be one with her.

“Ready?”

Such a loaded question. Was she ready to give herself completely to a man she’d once thought of as a childhood best friend, a man whom she’d spent years bickering with, believing he disliked her, a man she suddenly realized she was so attracted to and connected with that nothing else mattered in that moment except being close to him? Giving all of herself to him?

She nodded, and a cry escaped her as he entered her.

Domenico groaned. “You are so perfect.” He slid in and out, slowly at first, then faster, and harder, until she was panting and begging beneath him.

“Dom, Dom, Dom…” She moaned and

writhed, holding his hips against hers and rocking with his rhythm as he went deeper and deeper. “Dom, don’t stop.”

He moved faster, harder, pumping in and out of her with an intense urgency as though he needed to own her, take full control of her body.

He had it. “Oh God, yes.” She let her head fall back as her body trembled beneath him.

She was so close already—just from the feel of him moving in and out of her while his hands gripped her hips and his mouth kissed along her neck, her chest and over her breasts.

It had been so long. Her body was telling her just how much she’d deprived herself of this pleasure with its incredible desire for release. But it was also so much more than that.

She stared up at him. At Domenico Kasa.

In that moment, she knew what her heart had always known. He was the spark she was craving and missing. He’d been the source the entire time. Giving in to him, surrendering to these feelings, was the only thing she could do. The only thing she wanted to do with her entire body, mind and heart.

His gaze met hers and held—deep, hard with the passionate intensity of a lover waiting a lifetime for this connection. For this moment in time.

She gripped his arms as she felt him explode

inside her and her own ripples of orgasmic pleasure following seconds behind. She arched her back and pressed her hips into his as she felt him plunge deep one last time. His body shook above her, and she held on tight as the intensity of the orgasm brought her release like none she'd ever felt before.

As though this physical release was the manifestation of a lifetime of repressed feelings that were finally free to be communicated, explored…and reciprocated?

Satiated and spent, Domenico slowly slid out of her body and lay next to her on the bed. He immediately pulled her to him, and she cuddled into every curve of him, enjoying the sensation of being so close, so intimate…so safe and secure.

So sure.

That should have been a terrifying feeling, yet it wasn't. Not even a little bit.

He brushed her hair away from her face and kissed her gently on the forehead.

"That was…unexpected," she whispered.

"Unexpected, but also as familiar as if it had been destined to happen."

Surprised that he felt that way too, she pulled back slightly and looked into his eyes.

"I feel it all now—the attraction and connection I've always had for you and with you. I feel it all. I feel you," he said.

And her heart felt it all too.

Adriana rested her head on Domenico's chest and traced her finger along the sculpted muscles. Domenico gently kissed the top of her head, and she cuddled in closer to him. "Did you always know you wanted to be a professional tennis player?" She remembered him playing as a kid and being good at it, but she didn't remember it ever being something they talked about in depth back then.

"My dad always knew. Took me a little longer to get there."

"He encouraged it?"

"*Encouraged* is a mild way to put it." Domenico paused, trailing a finger along her arm. "Our father was a visionary—a very smart businessman who believed your best chance at success in life was to play to your skills. He was both charming in the right situations and cutthroat in the right situations. That's how he got ahead in this competitive tourism industry. And he enforced that same mentality and belief system on Leo, Mario and me."

Adriana gazed at him as he spoke, afraid to say anything or interrupt for fear he'd stop talking. Domenico rarely opened up. He'd always been the most quiet, reserved Kasa brother, even as a kid. It meant something that he was sharing all this with her. Obviously their physical intimacy had meant enough to him to have him opening up on another level.

"Anyway, the summer was not about relaxing or goofing off in our household. It was an opportunity to either learn the business by hanging out with him and our mother at one of the resorts or going away to some kind of camp. Leo and Mario always opted for the resort, but I chose different sports camps. Turned out I was a natural at tennis, so my dad decided we'd go all in on that. He saw that I wasn't as interested in operating the resort chain as the others were, so he said, 'tennis—that's your new passion'… and I didn't have an alternate solution, so…"

"Tennis was your new passion."

He shifted on the bed, pulling her even closer. "Exactly. Look, did I always love it? No. It was grueling training to be the best, because only that option existed for a Kasa. But it gave me a fantastic career. I have no complaints."

Adriana nodded. It had to be tough to be work so hard for a dream that you didn't fully want. But she knew Leonardo Sr.'s intentions were sincere. He saw potential in his son, and Domenico benefited from the intense, strict support from his father.

"What about you?" he asked in her long silence.

"Tennis might not have been my calling," she said teasingly.

Domenico tickled her, and she laughed and wiggled away. He stopped and drew her immediately back into his arms. "I meant, was running the restaurant, becoming a chef at Bellarini's the only dream you had for yourself?"

Adriana nodded. The only one she would share, at least.

Domenico pulled back and studied her. "No, it wasn't. Spill it. What did you want to do?"

"It was silly." He might have opened up, but his childhood dream career had transpired. She hadn't even attempted hers, and she'd never told anyone about it.

"Doubt that," he said gently.

Adriana sighed. "I wanted to be an F1 driver," she said, and waited for him to laugh or make fun.

Domenico's face took on a pensive look for a moment. Then he nodded. "You would have been good at that."

She pursed her lips and swatted at him.

"No, you really would have. You're skilled with your hands. You have sharp reflexes and reaction skills, and I know you like speed. You're fearless…"

She scoffed. "Hardly."

He propped himself up on his elbow and turned to look at her. "You are. I saw how you handled things when your dad got sick. No one else knew what to do or how to handle him. That stubborn old man refused to listen to anyone… and your father was a very intimidating man. You stood up to him and made him realize he needed to get help. That's fearless."

Adriana swallowed hard. That had been one of the toughest, scariest things she'd ever had to do. No one ever went up against their father—not her grandparents, not her mother, not Alex. When he'd gotten sick with dementia, no one had the courage to tell him he needed to take a step back from the restaurant—after nearly accidentally burning down Bellarini's—but she'd done it. And when he'd voiced his concerns about her taking over the restaurant, insisting maybe it should be Alex, she'd fought back then as well. And she refused to let her recent lack of confidence make her question his ultimate choice.

"I didn't think you were really paying attention to all of that."

"You and Leo were a thing. Believe me, I paid attention a lot. More than I should have."

"Trying to protect Leo—from my ill intentions." She knew he always worried that she was latching on to a Kasa for the financial benefits.

Maybe it was because he sensed the lack of true connection between her and Leo and that made him hesitant to trust.

"Partly. But not entirely."

Domenico stared into her eyes, and Adriana's chest tightened. The conversation turning to Leo brought the fact that she was in bed with her ex's brother to the forefront of her mind again. "Speaking of Leo…"

Domenico sighed and rolled onto his back. "Speaking of Leo…"

"This would hurt him, wouldn't it?" It wasn't really a question.

Still, Domenico nodded, confirming it. "This would hurt him."

Great.

Domenico pulled her closer, and she rested her head against his chest. "But not exploring this connection between us would hurt us."

She sighed. He was right, but could they selfishly allow themselves the happiness of spending time together—even though it can't last?

# CHAPTER NINE

It had to be the hottest day on record so far that year. There wasn't a cloud in the sky, and only the faintest of breezes blew every other minute as the Kasa resort staff set up for the staff-versus-guests beach volleyball tournament. Eight teams—four comprised of executive staff and four made up from guests who'd registered to participate—would play one another with the winning team gaining a point. Leading teams would play off in semifinals and then finals.

Leo stretched a few feet away. As Domenico approached, he fought the guilt of having sex with his brother's ex the night before. This morning it was all he could think about. The image of her was burned in his memory, and their agreement to keep this whole thing casual, just a fling, was torturing him. It was smart. It was the right thing to do. But damn, he couldn't shake the desire for it to be more than that. Yet he wasn't sure he was capable of fully trusting her.

He cleared his throat as he stopped next to his

brother and started mimicking his movements, stretching his hamstrings. "How did it go on the mainland? Linen crisis averted?"

"Turned out it wasn't even our order that got messed up. Total waste of a trip."

Not entirely.

Domenico nodded and cleared his throat again. "Hey, Leo…" He wasn't exactly sure what would follow, but he was desperate to get a gauge on his brother's level of attraction to Adriana. Whether he was actually still holding out hope for some kind of future together or if he was really fine with just being friends as he claimed…and maybe how he'd feel if Adriana started a new relationship. "You and Adriana dated for what? Four years?"

"Six."

Domenico turned around to the sound of Adriana's voice answering the question, and immediately his body sprang to life.

Adriana stood there wearing the sexiest sporty bikini he'd ever seen. It was, in fact, the Kasa de Paradise logoed bikini that all of the staff would wear that day to compete in the volleyball tournament, but Leo's "holy hell" was the only way to accurately describe how it looked on Adriana's body. Her curves made the thing look lethal.

Good thing she was on the staff team. Otherwise she'd be a massive distraction to Domenico's game. Not that they'd actually win—corporate rules were that guests always won. But they still liked to make their opponents work for it so they at least didn't feel the game was entirely rigged.

"Hey, Dom—close your mouth," Leo said with a grin.

"Ready to lose?" a female voice said behind him.

He turned to see Pricilla in a modest one-piece and matching sun visor. She smiled politely with a hint of cocky competitiveness.

"Bring it, Mrs. C," he said, embracing the spirit of competition and trying to ease the sting of his rejection the day before. Maybe they'd finally reached an understanding. Maybe she realized her actions had been inappropriate, and he'd simply been setting some boundaries.

She moved closer. "Oh, I intend to, darling," she said, and slapped his butt. "See you in the finals," she called over her shoulder as she sauntered away.

Okay, so maybe not.

Linda appeared on the beach, and he forced all thoughts of both other women—Adriana and Pricilla—out of his mind as he turned toward her. She was wearing flowy pants and a loose-fitting tank top, and he frowned. "Not going to play?"

Linda laughed. "My beach volleyball career ended before it began, honey." She gestured to her thin frame. "Not exactly the sporty type."

"Well, you're in for a fun time regardless. This competition is always a tense one," he said as she took a seat in a lounge chair and prepared to spectate.

"These loungers are the most comfortable beach furniture I've ever sat in. Only thing missing is a..."

Her words were cut short as a resort staff member arrived with a drink for her. She laughed as she gratefully accepted it.

"You were saying?" Domenico asked with a grin.

He loved his staff. The team members not participating in that day's events would be circulating refreshments to the spectating guests, keeping the players hydrated and playing DJ and motivators to keep the energy on the beach high all afternoon.

He nodded toward his team. "Gotta go strategize."

Linda nodded, already enjoying her drink. "Good luck!"

Domenico joined Leo, Adriana and other employees making up the staff team. They huddled up, and he deliberately avoided Adriana's eyes as he gave instructions to the team, naturally taking lead as the professional athlete in the group.

"Marco and Bella, you two are our beach volleyball pros, so naturally you'll team up. Lorenzo and Sofia, you're both completely new to the sport, an easy win for the guests. Leo, you are our top server, so you'll take that position. And let's partner you with Sofia. I'm fast, so I can work both sides of midcourt as needed..." He paused as he finally glanced at Adriana. "You'll be with me near the net..." In front of him, where he could stare at her perfect butt all game.

She nodded.

"I want Adriana to play with me," Leo said, turning to Sofia. "No offense, Sof. Adriana and I just used to play together all the time, so we make a great team."

*Yeah, a million years ago. Quit living in the past, Leo!*

Sofia shrugged. "All good. Dom, guess it's you and me?"

Guess he didn't have a choice. Making a fuss over it would raise all kinds of flags. Besides, Adriana was avoiding his gaze, too, and it was killing him not knowing what she was thinking—if she was regretting the night before or just playing it cool in front of Leo.

"On three," Leo said, putting his hand in the

center. Sofia's went on top of his, then Adriana's. Domenico stared at the pile of hands a moment.

"Come on, Dom," Leo muttered, misreading his hesitation.

He placed his on top of Adriana's, and immediately electricity coursed through his arm.

The others joined in.

"One, two..."

"Go team!" the others said as they broke away.

"Right, go team," Domenico mumbled awkwardly as they made their way onto the sand.

In position at his court, he glanced across the net, where their opponent guests had taken position—Pricilla as midcourt point like himself. Obviously confident in her volleyball skills.

The competitive streak in him peaked, but then, across the beach, Adriana bent her knees slightly and got into position in front of Leo. His brother's look of appreciation made his pulse race for a different reason.

The matches started. To say Domenico looked like he'd never played a sport a day in his life would be an understatement. His concentration was shot as his attention was constantly diverted from his game to the interaction between Leo and Adriana on their court.

Laughing. Fist-bumping. Chest-bumping. Butt-slapping.

Domenico was losing his ever-loving mind.

The sound of Adriana's laughter drifting across the beach, the familiar interaction between her and his brother, the fun they seemed to be having was making him full-on jealous. A rare feeling for him. One he didn't like.

Naturally his team did not advance to the finals.

Leo and Adriana did. Against Pricilla and a stock broker who was clearly a professional volleyball player in a former life.

Domenico collapsed into a lounger next to Linda, and a resort staff member handed him a drink.

Linda peered at him over her sunglasses. "Looked like you'd never seen a volleyball before."

Domenico laughed. "I was definitely off my game. Maybe don't mention it in your review."

Linda grinned. "I report what I observe. Good thing those two are fire!" she said, nodding toward Leo and Adriana.

Domenico's gaze landed on them, and his heart raced. They did work well together as a team. They were great friends and had a history. They had chemistry and love. Was there still something there?

His gut twisted at the thought as the final match began.

The music got louder and more up-tempo, and

resort staff and guests watched with intense interest as the game was played. Evenly matched and exciting…up until the last point, when Leo made a deliberate miss and Pricilla and her partner won. The two celebrated like they'd won gold at the Olympics, and Leo and Adriana were gracious in "defeat." He watched as the two of them shook hands with the winners and then shared a secret smile.

He couldn't take any more. All day, Adriana had barely looked at him. She hadn't said a word, and her interaction with Leo had Domenico literally feeling sick in the stomach.

He pushed up from the lounger. "Excuse me, Ms. Frank. Enjoy the medal ceremony. I have a few things I need to attend to." He walked away down the beach toward his hut, the sound of laughter and fun drifting on the breeze behind him.

He didn't look back.

Her silver Kasa de Paradise beach volleyball medal around her neck, Adriana scanned the beach for Domenico.

Where'd he go?

The rest of the staff and the guests were enjoying the music and refreshments, but he was gone. She sighed. During the afternoon, it had been so hard to stay focused on the game and keep things casual around Leo when all that was going through her mind was whether or not Domenico regretted their evening before…and whether he wanted a repeat.

She did. Desperately. But unfortunately, she already knew their pact to keep the attraction to a one-week-only fling was going to be impossible, for her, at least. Their time together—their intimacy—the night before had changed things.

"Close game," Pricilla said, approaching her. Her gold medal proudly on her neck, she'd been strutting around like a peacock. It took all of Adriana's strength not to admit they threw the game.

Guests were the priority.

Even snobby, rich, annoying ones.

She forced a smile. "You're quite the volleyball player. I take it you've played before?"

"I was a division champion in a lot of sports." She glanced across the beach, where her husband was asleep in a hammock. "So was he at one time—can you believe that?"

"That's how you met? Through sports?" she asked.

Pricilla nodded. "We had the same track coach in college. We were quite the couple back then."

The note of wistfulness in her voice gave her the briefest rare moment of sincerity. Adriana almost felt bad for her. Couples often grew apart as life happened. Maybe that's what happened with the Conways.

"Well, I'm sure he'll be happy to see that medal around your neck," she said.

Pricilla removed it, and her frosty demeanor returned. "It was just a silly game, honey."

Pricilla sauntered away, and Adriana sighed. A hint of humanity had been so close.

Leo approached and wrapped an arm around her shoulders. "We totally had them," he whispered.

She laughed. "We will always know the truth."

"Want to grab a drink?" he asked, looking at her expectantly.

Her gut twisted. That day must have felt like old times for him. Laughing, teasing, flirting a bit...but he had to understand that things were really over. Especially now. There was no way they could ever be together again after she'd been with Domenico. "Leo..."

He held up a hand. "It's okay. I get it." He removed his arm from around her and smiled. "Today was just...nice."

She nodded. "It was."

An awkwardness fell between them, and he checked his watch. "Guess I should shower and prepare for dinner too."

"I'll see you there," she said. Then she stood there as he walked away toward the main building.

She hesitated, eyeing the trail toward her guest room. Then her gaze drifted down the beach to a secluded, off-limits area.

Was he hallucinating? Had the heat that day given him heatstroke?

Domenico stepped off the steps of his beach hut and headed toward the water…where Adriana splashed in the surf.

"Water feels like heaven," she called out when she saw him on the sand.

"You're trespassing," he said, watching her. His heart raced, and he couldn't describe the relief he felt seeing her there. For the last hour, he'd fought irrational thoughts and images of her with Leo.

"Shut up and get in," she said.

He rarely swam in the sea, but in this case, he could make an exception.

For her, he was realizing, he'd made a lot of exceptions.

He removed his T-shirt and waded into the surf. "Feels a little cool," he said, taking in a sharp inhale as the water level reached his groin area. He sucked in a breath and plunged, refusing to look like a wimp in front of her.

He resurfaced beside her, instantly wrapped an arm around her waist and drew her into him. The scents of her coconut-flavored skin and floral hair reached his nose, and he breathed her in along with the salty ocean air. If someone could bottle this intoxicating aroma that embodied life on Kasa de Paradise, they could sell it in the gift shop and make a fortune—that smell of forever summer.

But then, it wouldn't be the same on anyone but Adriana. Her aura was what made it special.

His hands gripped her slippery wet waist, and he lifted her up onto his lap. She wrapped her legs around him as they continued to bob on the water. "What are you doing here?"

"You disappeared after the game awfully fast," she said.

"Bit of a sore loser," he said.

"Used to winning, huh?" she teased.

"In sports—yes. Besides, I didn't think you'd notice me leaving."

A slow grin appeared on her face. "Are you still upset that I partnered with Leo? Cause you could have fought for me."

He could have that day, but he didn't. Would he? When it truly mattered? He stared into her gorgeous eyes, and in that moment he knew he'd risk just about anything. "Choosing my battles, I guess."

She licked the salt-water droplets from her lips, and his body ignited.

She grinned, feeling his arousal. “Wow, doesn’t take much.”

His grip on her skin tightened, and he drew her even closer. “I wouldn’t say that. You are a lot of woman, Adriana.”

She shot him a look.

“You’re energy. You’re exuberant, unyielding energy, and this intoxicating physical prowess that you have—that’s what I mean.”

“Good save,” she said with a laugh.

That laugh.

When had it gone from irritating him to being a sound he cherished, lived for, couldn’t hear enough?

She lay back. Keeping her legs wrapped around his waist, she slowly lowered her body into the water, letting her hair float like a halo all around her.

She was no angel. She knew exactly what she was doing. In that position, her stomach was long, toned and lean, and the view of the underboob beneath that tiny bikini top was driving him mad.

He reached out. Placing a hand below her back, he forced her upright, then he stood and headed for shore, her body still wrapped around him.

“Hey, I wasn’t done in the water,” she teased.

“You’re done in *this* water,” he said, carrying

her across the sand, up the beach and straight toward the outdoor shower on the outside deck. He gently lowered her to the wooden planks and reached for the taps behind her.

Cold water sprayed from the faucet above. Adriana's breath caught sharply as it cascaded down her back.

Domenico adjusted the dial until warm water flowed. He stepped in under the spray along with her and placed a hand on her hip as he drew her into him. He lowered his head to hers and kissed her gently but with intention.

After all the torturous teasing he'd endured that day watching her with his brother, he needed to reclaim her—every inch of her.

A soft moan escaped her lips, making him instantly rock-hard. That simple little sound had him feeling like a god. The idea that his kiss, his touch could generate that vulnerable sound of pleasure from the most beautiful set of lips he'd ever tasted had his ego doing back handsprings and gave him all the confidence in the world to make her feel amazing.

He gently slid the fabric of the bikini straps down over her shoulders, down her arms, exposing her breasts as the fabric fell to the wooden planks at their feet. He swallowed hard, taking in the sight of the perfectly round mounds, the erect nipples aching to be touched, teased, kissed…

Holding her still pressed to him, their lower bodies connected, he cupped one breast and squeezed—gently at first, then more roughly. His thumb rolled over the hardened bud, flicking the nipple, then pinching gently…harder, and then a little harder.

Adriana moaned and wrapped one arm around his neck, forcing his head down toward it.

*With pleasure.*

He took the nipple into his mouth and sucked and flicked his tongue over it. His teeth grazed it. Her grip on his neck tightened and her back arched as she drove her body even closer to him.

He moved to the other breast and savored the taste of her coconut-flavored, salty flesh.

Adriana's breath was labored, coming in pants as she lowered her other hand down his abs and slipped it inside his wet swim trunks. Her hand wrapped around him. He growled against her nipple, pulling it with his teeth.

Her grip on him tightened as she started stroking the length of him.

Driving him wild.

He pulled away from her breasts and slid his fingers inside the fabric on her hips. He lowered the swimsuit bottoms down over the sexy curves as the water cascaded over her. He bent on his knees in front of her as he lowered the fabric down her legs, placing kisses along the beautiful skin as he went. She stepped out of the bikini bottoms, and he dropped them next to the bikini top on the wooden planks.

Starting at her ankles, he trailed his fingers upwards over her calves, the backs of her thighs…until both hands cupped her butt. He drew her hips forward and buried his head between her legs.

Adriana's head fell back and her hands tangled in his hair as she widened her stance to give him better access.

"Amazing," he murmured against her.

Holding her to him with one hand, he slid the other between her legs, inserting two fingers inside her wet body.

Adriana's fingers in his hair pulled gently. "Domenico… Dom…"

The desperation in her tone made his entire body come to life with desire—an intense need to have her, but more a determination to please her, make her say his name in that way over and over.

Her panting grew louder, and her legs on either side of him trembled slightly.

No way was she coming that quickly.

He gently moved his head away and got to his feet. He kissed her thoroughly, allowing her to taste herself on his lips. He lifted her, and she wrapped her legs around his waist. Then he pressed her up against the wall of the hut. He looked deep into her eyes—seeking permission, searching for hesitation.

"It's okay. I want this. I want to feel you inside me," she said.

That was all the permission he needed to bury himself deep within her. He moved in and out of her. She gripped his shoulders, her nails digging into his flesh. Panting, moaning, desperate to feel him fill her.

He plunged deeper and deeper inside her, his desire for her only increasing as he neared the edge.

"Adriana…"

"Please, Domenico."

The sound of her begging rivaled the sound of her laugh and the sound of her saying his name. He didn't know what made him more crazy for her.

"Adriana…" He moved back slightly and stared into her eyes, teetering on the edge, desperate with need.

She nodded, the lust in her expression nearly killing him.

He moved in and out of her several more times and felt his orgasm bearing down on him. He moaned as he fought to delay his release until he knew that Adriana was with him.

Adriana clung to him. "That's it, Domenico…

Yes, more…" she said, a pleading desperation in her voice.

She clenched her muscles around him as she ground her hips into him. He lifted her hips up and down as she clung to him, her breathing and moans growing louder in his ears as they reached their climax together. Her body sagged and he held her tighter as they fought to catch their breaths, spent and satiated.

"Adriana you are so incredible," he murmured against her lips, kissing her.

"You make me feel incredible," she said.

He slid out of her body and gently lowered her to the wooden planks. He reached for the soap and lathered her body. Taking his time over the sensitive areas.

She did the same. Moments later, after rinsing off, he turned off the water, and they went inside the room.

Domenico closed the door, feeling his body already coming to life once again. His need for her was unlike anything he'd ever experienced before.

When he turned to see her on the bed, the look in her eyes told him she was ready for him again too.

This woman was incredible. And there was no question—Leo could have her as a volleyball partner, but Domenico would fight for her when it mattered.

* * *

A wineglass in hand, showered and in fresh, clean clothing, Adriana walked around the villa later that evening after spending the afternoon in the kitchen on dinner prep. She looked at Domenico's tennis trophies on display. "You did have a very impressive career."

On the sofa, Domenico, dressed in a pair of shorts and sweatshirt, looking casual, comfortable and relaxed, stretched his arms along the back as he nodded. "I put in the work. It paid off."

"Why did you really quit playing professionally?" Adriana asked, joining him on the sofa. She curled her legs under her as she sipped her wine.

"Well, I could say it was because Dad was sick and Mario and Leo needed my help with the business...but truth is, I was becoming a dinosaur. Every year there were younger, faster, better players arriving on the courts. Can't compete with youth."

Adriana sent him a shocked look. "Humbleness? From the great Domenico Kasa?"

Domenico laughed and pulled her onto his lap so she was straddling him. "I told you, I'm not the arrogant guy you think I am," he said, gripping her hips and staring into her eyes with unconcealed attraction.

"I'm starting to believe it." She toyed with the strings on his sweatshirt. "Teaching here on the island is enough for you?"

Domenico sighed. "Not really, but I have to face facts. And my success did help in bringing in guests in the early days."

Adriana grinned. "Ah, there's the confidence..."

Domenico tickled her, and she wiggled to escape. "Stop, I hate being tickled," she said through her laughter.

"I know. I remember," he said, reluctantly stopping.

She stared at him. Their gazes locked on one another. "Look, I don't want to spoil the mood. I'm having a really great time with you this week...but are we going to tell Leo?"

Domenico hesitated and looked slightly pained.

She was assuming there was a need to. That this would be something they continued doing. But maybe this was just a weeklong fling for him—something he had no intention of pursuing once she returned to the mainland.

"I mean, we probably don't need to as it was just this week..." She desperately hoped she sounded casual as she stared into the red liquid in her wineglass, avoiding his gaze.

"Is that all it is?" he asked.

Was he disappointed? Or relieved?

The unreadable Domenico was back.

"Yeah… I mean, that's what we agreed to, right? You're here full-time on the island. I'm on the mainland full-time, so it's not like we can continue this—whatever this is…"

"Can't we?"

Another question instead of an answer! Infuriating Domenico was back!

"I'd like your thoughts on it," she said calmly, though her mind and heart were racing. They'd gotten close again that week and she'd let her guard down. She'd opened her heart to him—to the possibility of them—again but that may have been a mistake. If he really only saw this as a week-long fling and then went back to the Domenico that barely acknowledged her, it would destroy her.

Domenico put his wineglass down and looked serious as he said, "I think this week has been—enlightening—for us both, and there are some things that make this—whatever this is—complicated."

She nodded and waited, but that seemed to be all he was going to say on the topic. Complicated. He was leaving off there with no suggestions for a resolution to this complicated scenario they found themselves in.

That said it all, really.

She downed the liquid in the glass, climbed off his lap and stood. "I should call it a night." She reached for her things, and Domenico reached for her. He wrapped an arm around her waist and drew her back down onto his lap.

"Hey," he said.

She refused to look at him. There was no way she was going to let him see she was upset that he wasn't willing to try to figure this out, that it really had just been a week of passion for him... That's really all it might ever be. All it ever could be.

A tightness gripped her chest, and a desperate need to escape before Domenico could see he'd gotten to her sent her into flight mode.

But he refused to loosen his grip on her. "Hey," he said, gently tilting her face to look at him.

She kept her gaze lowered to his chin.

"Hey," he said again.

Adriana slowly lifted her gaze to his.

"Where are you going?"

"To my room. Another early morning."

Domenico sighed, searched her expression. He looked uncertain what to say. "You seem upset."

Way to read the room, Dom!

Adriana shook her head. "Nope. Not at all."

Domenico studied her. "Look, I..." He paused. For a long time.

Oh, this was torture! She needed to get out of there. With as much of her ego and heart intact as possible. She reached for his hands on her waist and slowly lifted them off her. "Dom, it's totally cool. We're good. There's nothing to figure out. As you said, things are complicated, and there's no point trying to complicate them even further." Each word stuck on her tongue as she said it, the way a lie used to when she was a kid.

Guilt glue, her mom had always called it.

"Adriana…just stay the night."

No way. Her pride was far too strong for that. "I'm going to call it a night, but I'll see you tomorrow." She kissed him gently and quickly. The kiss of someone desperate to go all-in but being forced to retreat out of self-preservation.

Domenico stood and reached for the island cruiser keys. "Give me a sec. I'll drive you back."

She shook her head quickly. "No, it's a beautiful night and still early. I'll walk." Adriana opened the villa door and glanced back over her shoulder. "Night, Dom."

"Night," he said as she closed the door.

Outside, she took a deep breath, feeling only more tightness in her chest as she exhaled. She headed down to the beach, and a heavy disappointment settled in her gut when it became clear he wasn't going to follow.

# CHAPTER TEN

THE LAST OFFICIAL night on the island for that week's cohort of guests was formal night—a favorite and highly reviewed evening that featured an elegant six-course meal, champagne and the glitz and glamour of Hollywood complete with a red carpet and photo opportunities.

The main building's dining room was elegantly decorated with white-and-black decor throughout featuring pressed, white linens covering the tabletops and chairs. Large crystal chandeliers had been hung, creating a kaleidoscope effect in the room as the crystals caught the light from hundreds of candles positioned throughout the room—the only light adding ambience and a romantic vibe.

Waitstaff dressed in black tails served meals to the beautifully attired guests, who all seemed relaxed and happy, though maybe a little sunburned and having overindulged after their week at Kasa de Paradise.

Adriana sat at the guest of honor table with the

Kasa brothers and Linda Frank, and the vibe was slightly tense at the table. Not that Linda or Leo noticed. The two of them had completely hit it off that week and were chatting like old friends across from her. But whenever her gaze drifted to Domenico, he was always staring at her. With this questioning look that she knew was asking if things were okay? If they were okay? If he'd completely messed up? And honestly, Adriana had no idea.

She hadn't slept well the night after leaving him in his villa and had found ways and reasons to avoid seeing him for the remainder of the week—hiding out in her room whenever she wasn't in the kitchen. He'd been putting out fires every day—a staff injury that needed a trip to the mainland hospital, an excursion cancellation due to weather that could have resulted in unhappy guests had he not scheduled an alternate activity, and other resort responsibilities—so he hadn't been around much either. They'd clearly both felt the tension the other night and both opted for space. Not communication.

Today she had been in full dinner prep mode, and he'd been overseeing the main building's dining room transformation. Therefore, they hadn't crossed paths. She'd at least expected to see him in the kitchen once that day as part of his overseeing everything, but he'd never shown up.

Looking at him now was killing her. Dressed in a tuxedo, he looked gorgeous—distinguished, handsome, and to everyone else, in control and composed. Only she could see the wheels turning in his mind. She knew he was thinking about this being their last evening together as much as she was and the way they'd left things unresolved.

All day as she'd worked, she'd been rehearsing what she'd say when they did eventually speak.

*Domenico, it was fun, and I'm happy that we reconnected and shared this special week together. One I'll always cherish.*

No more. No less.

He didn't need to know she was falling for him. He didn't need her asking how they could make this work or putting that kind of family pressure on him. And he certainly didn't need to be trying to communicate with her right now in front of the room full of people and at a table with Leo and Linda.

She frowned, seeing him make a motion with his head.

*What?* she mouthed.

He nodded toward the serving room where the next course was being prepped.

She hesitated, then set her fork down. She stood slowly and smiled. "Excuse me, I'm just going to check on the next course."

As she made her way across the room, she could feel Pricilla Conway's glare on her. That woman was far too perceptive, and she was not hiding the fact that she suspected something was going on between her and Domenico.

The woman wasn't wrong, and Adriana hoped she could keep it to herself for another twenty-four hours. As she reached the dinner prep room, she could see Domenico stand and excuse himself at the table.

Leo shot him an odd look. Then his gaze drifted across the room toward her.

His expression made her heart pound. A look of realization or at least suspicion registered on his face as his gaze shifted from her to his brother crossing the room toward her.

Uh-oh.

She shook her head at Domenico when he locked eyes with her. Jerked her head toward the restrooms instead.

He looked puzzled, and she jutted her chin toward their table, where Leo was still watching.

*Abort*, she mouthed as Domenico drew closer.

He frowned, and she sent him an exasperated look.

"Oh my God! Someone help! My husband!" Pricilla's shriek echoed throughout the ballroom.

All heads—including theirs—turned toward the commotion at the Conways' table.

Adriana was briefly glad for the interruption, until she saw Mr. Conway gripping his throat and struggling to breathe. Pricilla jumped up from her seat and continued to panic as Mr. Conway fell off his chair onto the floor.

From opposite ends of the dining room, Leo and Domenico rushed to their sides.

Adriana slowly approached, and the other diners all stopped eating and chatting to watch.

Including Linda Frank.

Leo grabbed his radio on his belt and spoke into it. "Medic required in main dining hall. Stat!"

Domenico knelt next to Mr. Conway. "Are you choking?"

Mr. Conway shook his head.

Dressed in a very short, very tight LBD, Pricilla bent next to Domenico—close. Inappropriately close, especially given the circumstances. "It's an allergic reaction. He's going into anaphylactic shock. Help him, Dom!" She clutched Domenico's arm like she was the one in distress, and he shrugged her off abruptly.

"Pricilla, please," he said, his tone short and sharp.

He was hot when he wasn't putting up with BS.

Leo didn't think so. He sent his brother a murderous look at the insensitivity. "Medic is on the way. Do you have his EpiPen?" he said gently to Pricilla.

Pricilla's red hair shook wildly around her shoulders. "No! We didn't think he'd need it! We filled out our guest profile, so I assumed the kitchen staff were competent enough to follow it." Her voice rose, and Adriana turned to glance at Linda, who looked slightly disappointed.

Other guests seemed uneasy as they eyed their meals and took in the poor man who continued to gasp for air, clutching his throat on the floor.

"Tell the medics to hurry! Please!" Pricilla shrieked.

Domenico turned to Pricilla. "What did he eat?" he said calmly.

Pricilla's expression switched from scared to angry as she glared at the half-eaten bowl of pasta on the table at her husband's spot. "This pasta! It must have had seafood in it."

Adriana glanced toward Linda again, who watched with a careful eye. Then she studied the food on Mr. Conway's plate. She shook her head. "No, there wasn't any seafood in this dish."

Pricilla advanced menacingly toward Adriana. "Then how do you explain this?" She motioned to her husband, who was now turning a very dangerous shade of red.

She didn't want to argue in an emergency, but she wanted the medic to know this might be more than an allergic reaction. "Mrs. Conway, I can assure you..."

"Maybe if you weren't preoccupied all week..."

What? Really, now?

"Pricilla, let's focus on your husband, okay?" Adriana's voice was calm despite her pulse throbbing in her veins. Being outed at this moment would be a disaster. And a man's life was at risk.

On the floor, Domenico looked ready to shut down Pricilla's implications. Leo sent the three of them questioning glances. Pricilla's cold, threatening gaze blazed into Adriana's, and she looked ready to burn the place down.

"Move aside! Make way!" The medic's arrival couldn't have come at a better time—for all their sakes. He gestured for everyone to move and crouched next to Mr. Conway as Domenico and Leo stood and backed away to give him space.

"Allergy?" The medic asked, opening his bag.

"Yes. Seafood," Leo said. "Presumably."

The medic quickly gave Mr. Conway an EpiPen injection. A second later, the man took a big breath, the panic instantly leaving his expression.

"Thank you," he croaked.

"He'll be okay," the medic told them, zipping his bag. "But we should probably bring him to the mainland hospital just to be sure."

Pricilla dropped to her knees and clutched her husband's hand, brushed his receding hair back off his sweaty forehead—barely hiding how disgusted she was by the act. "Darling, you scared me."

"I'm okay now," Mr. Conway said, looking surprised but eating up his wife's half-hearted all-for-show affection.

Pricilla turned toward Leo, Domenico and Adriana. "You almost killed my husband! We don't pay thirty-two thousand dollars a week to have our dietary restrictions ignored by…this…" She gestured insultingly at Adriana.

Domenico stepped forward. "Adriana says there was no seafood in this dish."

Leo looked at Domenico in surprise for coming to Adriana's defense.

Pricilla looked even more enraged. "Are you calling my husband and me liars?"

Across the room, at her table, Linda was taking it all in. Adriana gestured silently for Domenico to back down, to not make a scene. As heartening as it was that he was coming to her defense, they still had a review to secure.

Leo, also obviously desperate to appease Pricilla while saving the review, stepped in with a cooler hand and gentler approach. "No. Not at all. I'm sure there was a misunderstanding. We will launch an…"

Pricilla gestured to her husband's plate on the table. "Taste it!"

Leo shook his head. "That won't be necessary. As I was saying, we will..."

Pricilla picked up her husband's plate and shoved it toward Leo. Leo's spine tensed, his height growing an extra inch, and Domenico's hands clenched at his sides.

Both brothers now looked done with this over-the-top display from their guest. The Kasa family didn't do disrespect well and could only be pushed so far.

But Linda was watching, and after an immensely positive week, Adriana didn't want to see it all go wrong over this. Despite knowing she was in no way at fault, she stepped in. "I apologize, Mrs. Conway. Sincerely. I'll check with the kitchen staff right away to see if anyone might have added..."

Pricilla walked toward Adriana and dropped the plate of pasta. It shattered at her feet, making a mess all over the floor and Adriana's heels.

Domenico moved between the two women. For a moment, Adriana thought he was going to unload on the guest, but he touched Pricilla's shoulder gently. "It's been a very emotional, trying evening for you and your husband. We apologize for this. Let's call it a night. I'm sure

Mr. Conway could use your support as he gets some rest."

"I demand…" she started.

"All demands will be taken into consideration in a more formal setting once your husband has been thoroughly cared for." His tone was resolute—leaving no room for argument.

Pricilla looked enraged, but what more she could say in the moment? She stormed out of the dining room after her husband and the medic.

Leo and Domenico exchanged *that was a close one* looks, but Adriana's gaze was locked on Linda's disappointed expression.

"This is a disaster. We could have killed someone because of an oversight." Leo ran a hand over his face as he stormed into the office.

Domenico followed close on his heels. "Adriana says there was no seafood in that dish."

"And yet one of our guests almost died." Leo loosened his bow tie and undid several buttons on his dress shirt as he paced the office.

"Since when do you doubt Adriana?"

"Since when do you stand up for her?" Leo stopped pacing and eyed Domenico suspiciously.

"I just think we need to investigate this further before blaming her," he said slowly.

"You are the first one to say that guests are

always right—even when they are so blatantly wrong."

Domenico sighed. He hated when his brothers threw his own policies back at him. Especially this week when he was bending the rules. Or had been. Until Adriana seemed to vanish off the island whenever she wasn't in the kitchen. Since the night he'd regretted letting her leave his villa with things unresolved, his week had gone crazy with work demanding his time and attention, but he'd been desperate to get some time alone with her. There were things he wanted to say. He hoped the words would come to him in the moment. But she'd clearly been avoiding him, and time was running out. "In most all cases—yes, that's true," he said calmly. "But you know Pricilla Conway is vindictive."

Leo's eyes narrowed, and he looked even more accusingly at Domenico. "What exactly would she have against Adriana?"

Domenico looked away. "I don't know that she has anything against Adriana. I just mean that she's a bit obsessed with *me*, and maybe she assumed there was something going on."

"Why would she assume that?"

Was it hot in here? Felt like someone turned the heat up over the island by a thousand degrees. Sweat collected on his lower back under the tuxedo jacket and shirt, and he loosened the bow tie. "I don't know. I hang around the kitchen a lot… There was one morning I taught Adriana how to play tennis… Mrs. Conway saw…" Man, his mouth felt like a desert. Water. Water would be really great about now.

A look of realization dawned on Leo's face. "You've got a thing for her."

Domenico's awkward-sounding scoff got caught in his throat. "Mrs. Conway?"

"Come on, man, you know who I mean. You like Adriana. Is there something going on between you two?"

No. Nothing. Never.

Leo placed the palms of his hands on the desktop—his brother's tell when he was about to lose it—as he waited.

*Just lie.*

"Look, I wanted to tell you…"

Okay. Apparently, he was going with the truth.

"You're hooking up with my ex-girlfriend? When the reviewer is here?" The vein in his brother's forehead was pronounced and pulsing.

Hooking up? Sort of, but not exactly. *Hooking up* made it sound superficial, and despite his totally chickening out a few nights before when faced with the opportunity to tell Adriana that his feelings for her were real and more than just physical, this week had meant something to him, and he wanted to see her again. Often. However that looked or however they could make that work. It definitely wasn't hooking up. But they had in fact hooked up, so he was conflicted about the right answer here.

"It's not like that..."

"You *love* her?"

Uh-oh. Which one would be worse to Leo? A casual fling or real feelings?

"Okay, it's exactly like that—we're hooking up."

"You are unbelievable, Dom," Leo said, advancing toward him, his fists clenched at his sides.

Domenico refused to retreat even an inch. He didn't want to fight Leo, but if he had to, he knew he could kick his brother's butt. He hoped it wouldn't come to blows. They were both rational adults who could communicate like men. "Things have been over between you two for years."

"So that makes it okay? What happened to the bro code? We're actual brothers, so that makes this betrayal even worse." Leo's nose was inches from Domenico's chin.

"Hey, I could accuse you of it first. Adriana was my friend when we were kids."

"As you just said, you two were just *friends*. And we were *kids*. Hardly the same thing."

"I liked her."

"Then you should have made your move! Then *I* never would have, because *I* have this quality called loyalty." Leo's voice rose. He looked genuinely hurt.

Domenico's gut twisted in a knot. He hated arguing with his brothers, and he knew this time he was at fault for going behind Leo's back. He sighed and placed his hands on his hips. "Look, I'm not going to apologize for this connection between Adriana and me, but I do apologize for not talking to you first."

Leo's eyes narrowed. "Connection? So it wasn't just sex?"

Domenico shook his head. Confident Leo would have hit him by now if he was going to, he shoved his hands in his pockets and let his shoulders slump. "Believe me, neither of us expected this to happen."

Leo was silent for a long moment, his angry expression never dissolving as he took in the idea of his brother and ex-girlfriend together. Domenico waited, watching his brother's turmoil. At this point, he'd happily take a shot to the chin—prefer it over the anguish on his brother's face.

Finally, Leo took a step back and shook his head. "I trusted both of you."

That statement hit its mark.

Their partnership, their friendship, their brotherhood was all about trust and respect, and he'd lost both in his brother's eyes right now. Once lost, trust was hard to recover in the Kasa family. They forgave easily, but slights were never forgotten.

"Leo..."

Leo held up a hand as though to say *save it.* He'd clearly heard enough as he stormed out of the office and slammed the door behind him.

Alone in the kitchen, Adriana reviewed the recipes in that evening's menu. Not only did the pasta Mr. Conway consumed not contain seafood, none of the dishes did! There had been no seafood prep in the kitchen that day at all, and therefore no way that cross contamination could have occurred or an oversight could have happened.

Leo stormed in, and she glanced up at him. He looked stressed, annoyed and completely on edge, and she was desperate to put his mind at ease. Whatever happened to Mr. Conway was not their fault—not her fault. "Leo, I've been looking over all of these menus, and nothing calls for any kind of seafood."

"Maybe you made a mistake," he said coolly.

Adriana shook her head adamantly. "I didn't. You know me. I'm diligent, especially when it comes to food allergies. I reviewed all of the dietary restrictions the day I arrived. I was careful…"

"Well, maybe you got distracted."

Adriana caught the chilled tone and the implication of the words. She stilled as she set the recipes down on the counter. "What are you talking about?"

"By my brother."

His tone said he knew—he wasn't surmising or guessing.

Domenico told him? Why would he do that without at least giving her a heads-up? If things weren't serious and they weren't going to see one another after that week, why would he risk being honest with Leo over what was just a harmless fling? Why hurt Leo or put their working relationship in jeopardy?

Was there more to this week for him? Was that what he was trying to tell her that evening before the chaos and commotion started? There certainly was for her. Her heart raced, but then she saw Leo's hurt expression, and it plummeted to the depths of her stomach.

"I should have told you. I'm sorry, Leo…"

"I don't want to talk about it," Leo said, annoyance in his tone now. Which broke her heart in two. He cleared his throat and continued, "I just came by to tell you that you can leave in the morning."

He was dismissing her? "But you still haven't hired a permanent chef. I can stay a few extra days..."

"Not necessary."

"It kinda is," she said with a tight laugh.

"We can't afford more mistakes," he said. "Domenico was right. I never should have trusted you with something so important."

Adriana gaped as though he'd slapped her with the echo of her father's lack of faith. Leo had always been the one person she could count on to have her back and yet here he was morphing into a harsh critic she didn't even recognize. And while he might have defended her moments ago with Mrs. Conway, Domenico had been against her being there that week. She hoped she'd proven herself to him...but this fiasco might have just reaffirmed his belief that she wasn't a good enough chef for Kasa de Paradise.

Leo left the kitchen, and a devastated Adriana watched him go. She scanned the kitchen, tears burning the backs of her eyes, then gathered her Bellarini's recipe book and turned off the kitchen light as she exited for the last time.

Tired and defeated, Adriana packed her clothing into a suitcase an hour later. Disappointed in herself for hurting Leo and confused about where she stood with Domenico, she tossed things unfolded into the suitcase. Her gaze fell on the masquerade dress and shoes in the closet, and the memory of that night on the beach with Domenico made her chest tighten.

She had to talk to him before she left. Find out what had happened with him and Leo. Maybe get the courage to ask him what he'd been about to say earlier that evening. What had been so important that he'd wanted to sneak away from the dinner?

She didn't want to get her hopes up too high. Things might be quite different now after Leo's reaction to the news. It might have changed things for Domenico.

Did it change things for her?

A knock on the door made her hesitate before opening.

Domenico stood on the other side. His expression was tired, conflicted, but also held a trace of attraction and affection. Her shoulders relaxed slightly.

Adriana moved away from the door, and Domenico entered the room. He immediately reached for her and took her into his arms. She released a deep sigh as she sank into him. Despite the conflict she felt over Leo and the wrongful accusation by the Conways, being in his arms, breathing in the scent of him, sensing his strength and commitment to whatever was going on between them made her feel a bit better.

"Look, accidents happen. I don't blame you," he said gently, kissing the top of her head.

Adriana stilled and the peace she'd been experiencing vanished. "I didn't make a mistake. This wasn't my fault."

"Well, how did seafood get in the sauce?" He sounded pained that he had to call her out, and her frustration overtook all other emotion.

She freed herself from his embrace and backed away from him. She folded her arms across her chest. "I can't believe you believe her over me." But she could believe that he still doubted her, and that hurt.

Domenico stepped forward and reached out a hand toward her, but she shook her head. He sighed. "I'm sorry...but I asked one of the chefs to test the sauce left on Mr. Conway's broken plate. There was definitely seafood in Mr. Conway's pasta sauce."

"That's impossible! I reviewed all the menu items, went over all the recipes in the kitchen an hour ago—there was no seafood!"

"Adriana, I don't want to argue. It's done now. Mr. Conway will be okay. We will figure out how to recover from it if Linda's review isn't perfect. Let's just move on, okay?" He reached for her again, tried to draw her into him, but she held firm.

"Do you believe me?"

He ran a hand through his hair. "Adriana…"

Adriana trembled with anger and disappointment. Unbelievable. She nodded toward the door. "Get out so I can finish packing."

Domenico touched her arm gently. "Don't be like that. I'd like to stay with you."

"Why?"

"Because I…like you."

Like. Not love. And since when?

"Really? Cause according to Leo, you knew I'd mess this up. You never trusted me to run the kitchen in the first place. You never wanted me here." That all hadn't bothered her before, but it did now. So much.

Domenico sighed. "Look, I admit that at first, I was nervous, okay? But you proved me wrong. About a lot of things."

Was that supposed to make her feel better? Should she be grateful? "I'm glad I was able to be something unexpected for you. Please leave."

"Adriana… Leo knows about us."

"I know. He came to see me in the kitchen. A heads-up would have been nice, by the way." If they were going to hurt Leo by coming clean, they should have decided that together. Being blindsided like that hadn't been fair.

This was good. Anger was good—better than a broken heart.

"I didn't even tell him. He saw the way I was defending you..."

"Well, I don't need your defense." Adriana turned her back to Domenico and continued packing. She tossed a still-damp swimsuit into the suitcase and sighed. "I apologize about the review." The words were said through gritted teeth because she was sorry that the review would be negatively affected by that evening's drama, but she also knew it wasn't her fault. Not in the way he'd implied. It was their fault for not hiding their connection better in front of a vindictive woman who loved to hurt people because she was unhappy with her own life.

She heard Domenico move toward her and swallowed a lump in her throat when he placed his hands on her shoulders. She stilled, and a silence fell between them for a long, conflicted moment.

"I don't care about the review," he said. "Not anymore."

She knew the words were meant to make her feel better, but she knew they were BS. More importantly, *she* still cared about the review. Linda Frank mentioning this oversight would affect *her* and Bellarini's more than Kasa de Paradise. How could he not even see that? She whipped around to face him. "I do! Don't you get it? The rest of the review will be incredible, but the negative review of the food here this week is going to damage *my* reputation. It's going to hurt my restaurant too."

Domenico's expression hardened, and he let his hands fall away from her. "That's why you came. That's why you changed our menu. To get a glowing review for Bellarini's."

It wasn't a question, and she had no intention of hiding it. "My restaurant needed the boost, and Leo needed help," Adriana said, raising her chin defiantly.

"So you took a gamble on my resort?" Domenico stepped back.

She resisted the urge to move forward and reach for him. To reassure him that it hadn't been a gamble—she was a competent chef. Considering that evening, her argument lost a little footing, perceivably at least, but still, she refused to allow him to make her feel inadequate. "I don't see it that way, but if you do, then yes, I guess I did."

He leaned against the open patio door, lowered his head and took a deep breath.

"And us? What was that about?"

His gaze was downcast, and his body language was guarded. There was no way she was putting herself out there and telling him the truth about how she felt. What she wanted this week to have been about.

"I don't know, Domenico. You tell me."

Domenico finally looked up. His gaze met hers, and he stared at her.

Silent.

Neither of them spoke for a long, painfully awkward moment. Both daring the other to be the first to speak.

She was running out of air, but she refused to give in.

Suddenly, Domenico pushed off the patio doorframe and headed for the door. "Have a safe trip home." He left the room, and the door closed gently behind him.

Adriana watched him leave—her pride and conflicted heart preventing her from stopping him. Alone, she sat on the edge of the bed, sad and disheartened. "Damn it."

She eyed the suitcase and then the time on her cell phone. Her desire to flee overwhelmed her, and she stood and quickly packed the rest of her things. The last *Passage to Paradise* boat sailing for anyone needing to leave the island unexpectedly left in ten minutes. Technically this wasn't an emergency, but she knew Jon would take her back to the mainland tonight if she asked.

Therefore, Adriana boarded the *Passage to Paradise* eight minutes later.

* * *

Domenico stood on the sand outside his villa, watching the *Passage to Paradise* sail away. He knew Adriana was on it, and there wasn't anything he could do about it.

Yet this irrational urge to dive into the water and swim after the boat was overwhelming.

And then what? What would he say to her when he did catch the boat?

He'd had every opportunity to tell her how he felt moments ago in her room, and he'd let his pride and fear of being rejected prevent him from being honest about all the things in his heart. They'd agreed it was just a fling, and he'd once believed that she loved him only to watch her fall for his brother. He was terrified of fully opening himself up and committing to her now.

But the truth was, he'd fallen for her this week. Not fallen—fallen deeper—a part of him had always loved her.

As kids, that connection had been there, but through time, distance and separate life paths, they'd both pushed it aside. It had sat unacknowledged for so long.

This week had reopened his eyes to it. To the deep love he had for her.

These feelings had knocked him on his butt, then filled him with a sense of hope for a future he hadn't really thought was in the cards for him. And it might not be. Because he hadn't taken the chance.

As the boat left the narrows and disappeared in the light of the setting sun, Domenico turned and headed back toward his hut, knowing he'd just let the woman he loved sail away with his heart.

Linda, Leo and Domenico stood on the dock the next morning as other guests boarded the *Passage to Paradise*, relaxed, refreshed, sad to see their vacation on the luxury island resort come to an end.

Mr. and Mrs. Conway were already on board. Pricilla, wearing dark sunglasses and an oversized sunhat, refused to look toward Domenico.

She wasn't the only one. Leo had refused to look his way or acknowledge him at all that morning, and the tension between them had to be apparent to the reviewer. It lingered as thick as the heat in the sea air.

But if she knew something was off, she was professional enough to hide it. "Thank you both again for this incredible experience. Kasa de Paradise is really something—a true oasis on this coast."

Domenico handed Linda's suitcase to the boat captain and looked nervous as he said, "About your review..."

"Look, Dom. I can't ignore what happened at dinner last night." She paused, lowering her voice and sending a side-eye glance toward the Conways. "But I will consider the source of the complaint in my overall rating."

"I appreciate that. Thank you," Dom said gratefully. "We'd hate to have not lived up to our father's standards of guest experience."

"Please tell Chef Adriana that even with the mix-up or whatever it was…her food was the best I've had in years. It's too bad she had to leave early. Though the chefs were fantastic this morning."

Domenico avoided Leo's intense gaze on him as he nodded. "I'll be sure to pass along both compliments."

Linda boarded the boat and put on her sunglasses as she took a seat. "My review will be posted on the *Travel Island* website next week. I look forward to visiting again."

Domenico and Leo waved as the boat pulled away. Once Linda and the *Passage to Paradise* were out of sight, both men silently headed off in opposite directions.

# CHAPTER ELEVEN

BELLARINI'S WAS BUSY, bustling, chaotic. All of the tables inside the dining room were full, and there was a lineup of customers waiting for a table in the lobby as Adriana entered her family restaurant the following afternoon. She looked around.

Surprised and more than a little confused.

"Welcome to Bellarini's. Do you have a…" The hostess, Valentina, paused and smiled nervously when she glanced up from the reservation book and saw her. "Adriana! You're back early! We weren't expecting you in until tomorrow."

Adriana continued to look around the dining room—where every table was full. For lunch. On a Friday. "What's going on? Did someone reserve the restaurant for an event?"

Valentina looked slightly sheepish. "No…"

"Did one of the other restaurants close unexpectedly?" Was this divine overflow from someone else's misfortune?

"No."

"Valentina! Say more, please!"

Valentina shrugged and looked reluctant to embellish. "It's been like this the past four days."

"Really? Why?"

"You should talk to Alex," she said before scurrying away.

Adriana smiled at diners—unfamiliar new faces—as she headed further into the restaurant. She waved at several regulars as she made her way to the kitchen, but for the most part, she didn't recognize anyone. Where had all the new customers suddenly come from?

Her stomach knotted with unease.

*What did you do, Alex?*

Adriana pushed through the swinging door and entered the kitchen. Full staff on deck, scurrying to fulfill orders but in a surprisingly controlled and organized way as though they were used to this level of business. In the center of the commotion, Alex directed the sous-chefs and waitstaff expertly.

She scanned the dishes being prepped. Some she recognized. Others…

Her chest tightened. "Hey, Alex."

Alex turned and looked slightly panicked to see her. "Don't be mad," he said, speaking quickly.

Whenever anyone started any conversation with those words, it was never off to a good start.

Adriana folded her arms and raised an eyebrow. *Stay calm.* "What's going on?"

"I tried some of those new menu items I've been asking you to try…and, well, they've been a hit." Her brother looked proud despite knowing he likely annoyed her.

"A few new items have this place at full capacity?"

Not buying it.

"Okay. A lot of new items and a social media post or two…" Alex added a garnish to a plate and sent it out.

Adriana glanced at the familiar-looking entrée leaving the kitchen. Familiar but not quite a Bellarini's menu item. She could tell by the texture of the white cream sauce. "They don't look that different, but they definitely are." The kitchen even smelled different. Not bad. Not worse. Just…different.

And different was making her nauseous.

"That's the point. On the outside, they look like Bellarini's traditional menu, but the ingredients are different, some slightly healthier, some tweaked for a varied flavor or texture…"

Alex picked up a piece of garlic cheese bread from a tray and handed it to Adriana. "Try this."

Adriana stared at it with disdain. "If this is almond flour…"

"Just shut up and try it."

Adriana took a bite. She chewed slowly, waiting for the disgusting taste or at least chalky texture to land on her tongue, but it didn't. The bread was actually moist and soft…

Dared she use the word *delicious*?

What kind of witchcraft was this?

Aware of Alex's scrutiny, she shrugged casually. "It's okay…"

"It's more than okay. It's delicious. And carb-free. I can't make it fast enough." Alex reached for the rest of her bread, but Adriana sighed in annoyance and popped the garlic bread into her mouth.

"What else did you change?" she asked while chewing.

A sous-chef placed a dish on the counter in front of him. "Let's just get through tonight's service. Then we will talk, okay?"

Adriana looked ready to argue, but the extreme pace in the kitchen left no room. "I guess I don't really have a choice."

"Great. Well, in the meantime—grab an apron and get to work," Alex said.

Adriana gaped slightly. This was her kitchen.

Or at least, it was.

That day, her brother was in full command.

Her chest tightened as she scanned the kitchen. It didn't even feel like hers anymore. Gone was the easygoing vibe full of fun banter as everyone was laser-focused on the orders coming in. The dishes might look familiar but they were different and even the regular music had been replaced with a more recognizable Italian melody.

This restaurant was her entire life. She'd made so many sacrifices to keep it the way her parents and grandparents had…and now she wasn't sure she even belonged there.

But then, where did she belong?

The alternative—a life on Kasa Island—wasn't an option anymore. Domenico had made that very clear.

She suddenly felt like maybe everyone was right—that she wasn't good enough anywhere.

"Adriana! Let's go," Alex said, cutting into her thoughts.

Adriana sighed as she grabbed an apron and got to work.

Hours later, once the restaurant was empty and everyone had left for the evening, Adriana—exhausted by the intense pace that hadn't let up all day and into the evening—sat across from Alex in a booth. On the table between them were register receipts from that week and Alex's new menu. Adriana turned the beautifully designed menu over in her hands. "You did all of this in a week?"

"No. I've been working on it for a year." He took a sip of wine and sat back in the booth, looking relaxed, pleased, and more than confident and ready for this conversation.

She was not. After the week on Kasa Island with her heart and mind in constant turmoil, that unexpected day in the restaurant and this long-overdue discussion with her brother were the last things she'd been expecting to deal with.

"You really were hopeful I'd get on board with this?" To go through the trouble of having menus made? When did he even have time to get these printed? Clearly, a motivated Alex was an unstoppable Alex.

Alex took a deep breath and sat forward. "Actually, Adriana, I was planning on opening my own restaurant."

He was what? She dropped the menu and her bottom lip. She stared at him that way for a long moment, waiting for her brain to catch up.

"I made these menus months ago because I was considering a new place of my own," he said a little more gently, but still with determined confidence.

"Seriously? But this restaurant has been in the family for three generations. You'd just up and leave like that?"

Alex shook his head. "Not just like that. After years of asking you to consider making some changes. Some necessary upgrades and revisions. Asking you to at least consider my ideas. Ideas that I've just proven to work."

"Oh, come on, Alex. You had one great week. These crowds will die off."

"At least the restaurant wouldn't be a ghost town in the meantime."

Ouch.

Alex softened his tone as he continued, "I don't mean to offend, Adriana. You're a fantastic chef, but you have to realize that if we don't adapt, Bellarini's won't be around for a fourth generation."

Adriana sat back, considered her brother's words. She knew the menu was old, but it consisted of recipes that had been in the Bellarini family for decades. Each dish represented memories. Each taste, each smell…all brought back generations of good times together, eating as a family, laughing and talking into all hours of the night. They were more than just recipes.

But she couldn't argue that sometimes traditions didn't pay the bills.

And Alex had a right to forge his own path, start something he fully believed in, something he could be proud of the way she was proud of what they had right here—all around them.

"So, you're leaving? Starting your own place?"

"I don't want to. I want to implement these changes permanently here."

"What about my menu? Grandma's menu? The regular guests who love Bellarini's for what it currently is..." She stared at the new menu in her hands. Pain showed in her expression. "Was."

"I'm not suggesting eliminating the old recipes completely. Just offering both options. It's worked well this week. In fact, take a look..." He reached into a folder and produced a mock-up of a new Bellarini's menu with two sections, Traditions of Taste and Evolution of Flavor.

Guests could choose which they preferred.

It was a great idea. A way to move forward but preserve the past, but...

"Supply costs will double. The workload doubles..."

Alex nodded to the revenue numbers from that week. "We made more this week than we made in three months."

Adriana winced at the truth, and Alex touched her hand. "It's not your fault. New restaurants are adding to our competition all the time. We need to evolve or..."

Close up shop.

Adriana was silent for a long time. This was the right thing to do, but it was just so hard to do it. Not unlike so many other choices she'd faced that week. Leaving the island—escaping—without being honest with Dom had weighed on her all day. She should have at least told him and let things unfold as they would have.

Better to live with the knowledge that she'd gone after what she wanted than live with regret.

Same for the future of Bellarini's?

Finally, she reluctantly nodded. "Okay…we will try it your way for a while."

Alex looked relieved as he squeezed her hand. "Great. Because I'd hate to leave here. This is my home too."

Adriana scanned the restaurant, then studied the new menu in her hands, a look of uncertainty on her face.

She hadn't been brave enough to take a chance on her and Domenico, but she was determined to find the courage to save her family restaurant.

A few days later, Adriana sat on her cozy sofa across from Isabella. They had wineglasses in hand.

"I can't believe those jerks actually think you could be responsible for that guest's allergic reaction," Isabella said in appropriate bestie rage. Her friend was in her pajamas, having responded to Adriana's SOS text in record time.

"There was definitely seafood in the sauce, according to one of the chefs." Though she still had no idea how it could have happened. There had been zero reason to have any ingredients containing seafood anywhere near the food prep that day. She'd replayed the day over and over…

Isabella shook her head. "I'm not buying it. You're the most diligent chef I know."

"Thanks, friend." But Isabella was a ride-or-die. If Adriana hit someone with her vehicle, Isabella would claim the other person must have been at fault.

However…

Adriana sipped her wine and shot her friend a glance. "You should have told me about Alex making those changes."

Isabella looked slightly sheepish, but the other key quality in their friendship was brutal honesty. They always gave it to one another straight. No sugar-coating or enabling. "I'm sorry, but you saw for yourself how well it worked."

"The crowd the other day was hard to ignore." She stared pensively into her wineglass with a conflicted look. "I've agreed to try it Alex's way for a while."

"That's big of you. It is his family legacy too, and I think you need to trust him."

Adriana nodded. It wasn't that she didn't trust Alex. She was starting to feel like she couldn't trust herself. A new menu meant proving her skills as a chef beyond the Bellarini traditional recipes that she'd known how to prepare since childhood. And that week at Kasa de Paradise had only furthered her doubt in her ability to take risks.

She'd walked away from Domenico because of the uncertainty. The uncertainty of his feelings for her, the uncertainty of their ability to make a relationship work, the uncertainty of a future together. She'd thought that she'd gotten to know Domenico again—the real Domenico. But what if she'd just imagined it? Giving up and walking away instead of being vulnerable had seemed like the safest option.

Unfortunately, playing it safe left her with a struggling restaurant and an aching heart.

Isabella hesitated. "Have you talked to Dom?" she asked. Another bestie trait was being able to read Adriana's silence.

She shook her head. "Probably for the best. I think I drove a wedge between him and Leo, and for what?"

"The love of a lifetime?"

If she admitted that, her heart might shatter. Therefore, she scoffed. "Before this week, I could barely tolerate him."

"They say there's a fine line between love and hate." Isabella raised a suggestive eyebrow. "And you two did have a history of friendship."

"Well, he hasn't reached out to me." And they said if a man wanted to, he would. I mean, technically she wanted to and she wasn't, but that wasn't the saying. "Neither has Leo." And that made her feel a whole new level of sadness. She and Leo might not be meant to be romantically, but they were such great friends. She hated the thought that she could be losing him. He'd meant a lot to her their entire lives, and the hurt in his expression that night in the kitchen had made her feel terrible.

Though not as much as Domenico's refusal to believe her and fight for her, for them.

"Leo loves you, and even he knows deep down that you two were not right for one another. He'll come around," Isabella said gently, sipping her wine.

She hoped so. In the meantime, "I think the best thing to do is forget all about the Kasa brothers and their fantasy island." After all, she was going to have her hands full with the new Bellarini's menu.

"Can you do that?"

Maybe when she was so consumed with work, she wouldn't have as much time to think about Domenico and how much she missed him. The way he drove her crazy—in all the best ways. They way he'd looked at her as though he'd loved her forever. The way he made her body come to life with the simplest touch…

"What choice do I have?" she said with a sigh.

She'd already made a mess of things. She refused to make things worse.

A *Travel Island* magazine notification chimed on her phone. Adriana opened the app and saw the resort review posted. "The *Travel Island* review is live." Her hand shook slightly as her finger hovered over the link.

"Read it!" Isabella moved closer and peered over her shoulder.

"I can't. What if it is horrible?" Her knees bounced, and she thought she might be sick. She had been uneasy about so much since leaving Kasa de Paradise—the review not least of all. The Conways' incident was a serious one, no matter who was at fault, and she knew it wouldn't reflect well on the resort. It wasn't something Linda Frank could have overlooked.

"Not knowing won't make it better," Isabella said.

"You read it," Adriana said, handing Isabella the phone.

Isabella set her wineglass aside, clicked on the review link and cleared her throat. "A paradise on the coast—a review of Kasa de Paradise by Linda Frank."

Adriana held her breath as Isabella read.

"The experience on Kasa de Paradise begins with an unforgettable voyage on the…"

Adriana waved her hand. "Skip ahead… Look

for anything to do with the food." She couldn't sit through five thousand words of Linda's review right now. She'd read the full article later. She needed to know what the woman had said about her part.

Isabella hummed as she scanned. "Okay… here we go. Ready?"

No. She nodded.

"The food at Kasa De Paradise was everything indulgent and satisfactory. The kitchen, led by award-winning chef Adriana Bellarini, was well-run and served a variety of options to suit even the most expensive palate. Despite a mix-up in the kitchen and an allergy scare, Ms. Bellarini is destined for greatness with her abandonment of flavor restrictions, truly catering to those who appreciate luxury indulgences in all aspects of their vacation. With the combined elements of tradition and modern embellishes, Ms. Bellarini is a top chef—a treasure in any luxury resort kitchen."

Adriana released a sigh of relief and sank back against the sofa cushions.

"See. Destined for greatness…a treasure… This woman knows what's up," Isabella said, smiling proudly at her.

Adriana laughed as she nodded toward the phone. "Okay, read the rest of the review now." Her heart felt a little lighter as she settled in to listen, but she was only half paying attention as her mind wandered to Domenico. Had he read this yet? Would he reach out once he had? Once he saw that she hadn't completely sabotaged his resort that week?

And what if he did—what then?

Worse—what if he didn't?

# CHAPTER TWELVE

A BEAUTIFUL, SUNDRENCHED day settled over the island as new weekly guests enjoyed the resort's activities. Crew members moved about facilitating activities and tending to the grounds as Domenico hit tennis balls shooting out at maximum speeds from the Spinfire Pro on the other side of the court. He sent one ball after another flying across the net. Nothing was as therapeutic as whacking the hell out of the green spheres, but that day even the strenuous activity wasn't working to erase the thoughts and conflict about Adriana from his mind.

Mario appeared on the courts behind him and folded his arms across his chest as he leaned against the fence. "Looking a little sloppy."

Domenico ignored his brother as he kept on whacking the balls.

"Did you see the *Travel Island* magazine review?" Mario asked.

"Yep."

"Four and a half stars. Not bad."

"Not five," Domenico grunted. If that last incident with the Conways hadn't occurred, maybe they'd have received the coveted five stars from Linda Frank. He was holding on to that sense of blame and irritation with Adriana as fuel to keep from reaching out to her. For the last three days, she'd been on his mind constantly. Wherever he went, wherever he looked, there were reminders of her and their time together. She'd spent one week on that island, and yet she seemed to have permeated every inch of it. He saw her everywhere. He swore the scent of her skin had somehow become the island's new signature aroma.

And things here felt different now without her. Not as vibrant. Not as alive.

Mario sighed as he approached and turned off the machine. "You and Leo ever planning on speaking to one another again?"

Probably not.

In three days, they'd barely exchanged three words. What he'd done was wrong—in that he should have told Leo and not hidden it from him. But he didn't regret being with Adriana. And his brother being upset was understandable, but if Leo was being honest with himself, he didn't even really want to be with Adriana. Leo loved the bachelor life, the carefree freedom. He said so all the time.

So why did they both have to suffer? Didn't seem very brotherly.

"You guys are being jerks," Mario said, typing on his cell phone.

Domenico lowered the racket and fought for breath as he shot his brother an annoyed look. "Do you need something?"

"I need my brothers to stop acting like idiots so we can properly run a resort."

That would be ideal, but, "It's complicated."

"That what your Facebook status says?"

Mario's irritating grin was the last thing Domenico needed on his frazzled nerves and conflicted heart. Domenico moved around his brother to grab his towel. He wiped the sweat away from his neck and face.

"Look, man, Leo and Adriana were over a long time ago. They weren't right for one another."

"Tell that to Leo." His brother was the one hung up over Adriana. Had been for years. Not that he was making excuses for his behavior, but whether he and Adriana were together or not, she wasn't in love with Leo anymore.

"I did," Mario said.

"What did he say?"

"He told me to screw off."

Domenico flicked the machine back on and returned to hitting balls.

Mario shrugged as he started to walk away. "Anyway, I thought you should know that Mr. Conway's seafood reaction wasn't Adriana's fault."

What?

A ball flew from the machine and hit Domenico in the head as his attention swung to Mario. He mumbled a cuss word, rubbing his forehead and moving out of the line of fire. He approached Mario. "What are you talking about?"

"Housekeeping found a package of powdered shrimp in the Conways' room after they checked out. Hidden beneath the mattress."

The woman tried to kill her own husband? That was low. Even for her. "Are you serious?"

Mario shook his head. "Looks like Mrs. Conway was trying to eliminate her husband from the love triangle you three had going on."

Domenico shuddered at the thought. "There was no love triangle."

"Maybe not one that included Mr. Conway."

Mario was annoying. "So, you're saying Mrs. Conway put the powder on her husband's food? You're sure?"

"I mean, we can't prove it, so there's no point calling the police about it or anything, but it looks that way. Why else would she have something she knew her husband was severely allergic to in the room?" He paused. "I just thought you'd like to know that Adriana wasn't to blame."

"Did you tell Leo?"

Mario nodded and grinned. "He's groveling pretty good with six dozen roses being delivered to Bellarini's as we speak."

Of course Romeo was.

Domenico quickly packed up his tennis racket and headed off the court.

Mario called after him. "By the way, we still have an opening for a head chef!"

Adriana scanned the six dozen red roses on the counter in the kitchen of Bellarini's. She knew who they were from without having to read the card.

Leo.

Roses were definitely not Domenico's style.

She sighed as she read the card. *I should never have doubted you. Forgive me?*

He must have been happy with Linda Frank's review. It wasn't her coveted five-star, but it was very flattering, and she did highly recommend Kasa de Paradise. It was a relief that Leo had reached out. She'd been worried that their friendship was over. The thought had weighed heavy on her along with so many others.

She tucked the card inside the pocket of her chef's coat and retrieved her cell phone. She opened the text message thread to Leo and typed, Always...forgive me?

Three dots—typing...

She held her breath as she waited.

For falling for the wrong Paradise billionaire? I'll get over it eventually ;)

Adriana smiled sadly as she tucked the phone away and got to work.

Within moments of opening for lunch service, the kitchen was busy, food orders coming in one after another. A lot of orders were from the traditional menu, but quite a few were Alex's new recipe options and those Adriana struggled with.

Alex returned to the kitchen with an entrée barely touched. "Table fourteen is sending back the seafood lasagna. They asked for whole wheat noodles and half-fat cheese."

"Half-fat cheese. What's the point of eating?" Adriana grumbled. She took the plate from her brother and dumped the contents, then started over.

Dish after dish was returned...

"Who eats like this!" Adriana yelled in frustration after the fourth one.

Alex pulled her aside. "Hey... I know this is challenging, but get your head in the game."

"It's these choices! You're giving people far too many."

"It worked fine last week."

"It's not working now."

Sous-chefs and staff turned to look their way, and Alex dragged her into the walk-in freezer. Once the door closed behind them, he said, "You agreed to try this."

"I am trying." It was a lot to expect, especially with the crazy pace they were suddenly working at. As much as the business was good for profit, she missed the slower pace where she could really deliver on quality. She hadn't even had time to leave the kitchen to go greet guests—chitchat with the old regulars and tell the Bellarini's history to new ones. The other parts about working in a restaurant that she enjoyed. The personal touch and dining experience she knew brought guests back time and again.

This pace wasn't allowing her to operate the way she thrived. It was stressful, chaotic and not the career she loved. But it was only the first day, so she took a breath. "Familiarizing myself with the new recipes will just take some time."

Alex nodded. "Then how about letting me take the lead? Just until you're up to speed?"

The stubborn Bellarini streak in her awakened. Absolutely not. She was in charge. She was in control. This was *her* kitchen.

One she wasn't successfully running at the moment.

The realization that she was spiraling mid-lunch rush in the walk-in freezer hit her like a block of ice to the forehead. She had to admit that she simply couldn't do this yet. She did need time. Alex was already familiar with the new recipes, and she had to admit, his way of running the kitchen had been smooth and efficient despite the heavier workload. He was cool and calm under pressure.

She also had to reluctantly admit that her head just wasn't in the game since Kasa Island. Her thoughts were constantly drifting to Dom and their magical nights together on the island. The way he looked at her, kissed her, held her—her head and heart were a mess. They'd both said it was just a weeklong fling, and obviously that been true for him…yet that spark between them told her he felt something deeper too.

But she had no idea what to do about Dom…about them…or her restaurant.

Therefore, for the sake of Bellarini's, she fought her pride as she nodded. "You take the lead."

Leo sat at his desk, résumés for a new head chef in front of him, as Domenico entered the office. "Hey…" he started nervously.

Leo didn't look up. "I guess Mario told you about the Conways?"

"Yeah..."

This was awkward. They needed to start talking again. They couldn't continue to run a high-end luxury island resort without communicating. Besides that, they were brothers. They'd overcome worse than this, and he refused to let their complex feelings about Adriana come between them.

They both loved her. In different ways.

And neither of them should be without her.

One thing had become blatantly clear these past few days—Domenico *couldn't* be without her, so he had to somehow make this okay for Leo.

Domenico sighed. "Look I'm just going to say it. We need a new chef, and Adriana is perfect for the position."

Leo sighed as he looked up from the résumés. "I tried already. Years ago. She turned it down."

"That was before."

Leo looked up, a mix of amusement and annoyance in his expression. "You think you can change her mind? Make her give up her life on the mainland and her family restaurant—for you? *I* wasn't enough after years of dating, but after a week together, *you* are?"

Leo was not going to make this easy. The last

thing he wanted was to hurt his brother's ego, but he knew his connection with Adriana was stronger after one week than it had ever been with Leo. She'd felt that way too, but Leo didn't need to hear that.

Besides, it really wasn't about him, or at least not fully. "Not for me. But maybe for the opportunity to cook the way she loves to cook."

Leo frowned. "She has that now."

Domenico moved closer to the desk and lowered himself into a chair across from his brother. "No, she doesn't. Alex has been trying to change things. Implementing a new menu. Bellarini's isn't doing so well anymore. Or at least, it wasn't until last week, when Alex was running the show."

Leo stared at him. "Adriana told you all that?"

"Some of it." The not doing so well part. The rest he'd discovered by scrolling the Bellarini's social media page. The new menu was advertised, and videos of lines outside were posted. Alex's new way of doing things was working—at least for the restaurant's bottom line.

His heart ached for Adriana. It couldn't be easy implementing these changes. He knew she longed to see Bellarini's thrive for many more generations based on the way things always were…but change was inevitable.

He hoped maybe she'd consider a big one for

her own future, because in the recent days without her, she was all he could think about. He suddenly didn't want to spend his life making this resort a success without her by his side. The week before had changed things. Had changed him.

Leo dropped the résumé in his hand and sat back in the seat. "You two really got close?"

"I know you don't want to hear it, but yes. And I am sorry, man. I never intended to have feelings for her. You know that. Before last week, I thought I could barely stand being around her." He paced the office and ran a hand through his hair. "Turns out that tension wasn't exactly from hating one another…" He stopped pacing and turned to point a finger at Leo. "And really, this is your fault."

Leo folded his arms across his chest. "You've got three seconds to explain that before I punch you in the face."

Domenico reached for his cell phone and opened the message thread between them. He scrolled to the photo of all of them as kids. "You sent us this."

"It's a cute old photo."

Domenico handed Leo the phone. "Zoom in on my face." He waited while his brother did.

Leo peered at the image. Realization dawned

in his expression. Then he handed the phone back. He sat up in resolve. "All I know is that you have it bad for my ex-girlfriend."

"I do." No sense lying about it. He didn't want to. He wanted to shout his feelings for Adriana from the rooftop of the main building and let it echo all the way to her heart on the mainland. Admitting his feelings to his brother and seeing if this was something they could overcome was the first step.

Leo was silent for a moment. "Do you really think she'll consider the position?"

"Only one way to find out."

Leo let out a long, deep breath. "Then go get her, man."

Relieved, Domenico nodded and sat in the chair across from him. He had his brother's blessing to be with the woman he loved. A huge weight was lifted from him.

Leo gestured for him to leave. "Like—now. If you haven't noticed, we're in desperate need of a chef."

"Right," Domenico stood. He hesitated, then extended a fist toward his brother.

Leo stared at it, then grinned. "Not quite at the fist-bumping stage yet, bro."

"Understood," Domenico said with a grin, but knowing all was forgiven, he left the office with a clear head and determined heart.

* * *

The restaurant was closed and empty—all guests and staff gone for the night. The lights were dim, and only soft Andrea Bocelli music played as Adriana walked around the restaurant and looked at the pictures of her family on the walls. Memories the restaurant held came flooding back.

This was her history, her legacy, her life... What would she do without Bellarini's? But if she didn't adapt to the new menu and new vision for her family's business, there would be no future generations of families to feed at the restaurant. Her parents and grandparents had always worked so hard to keep the doors open, and Bellarini's was an important part of the culture here. She wouldn't let her own stubbornness and pride stand in the way of its future success.

Handing the reins to Alex that day had felt like failure. Defeat. She shouldn't feel that way. They were a team. But she couldn't shake the unease in the pit of her stomach that they were turning Bellarini's into something she soon wouldn't recognize.

A knock on the door caught her attention, and she turned to see Domenico standing outside the glass window.

Her heart stopped, then immediately started racing. What was he doing here? Leo had sent flowers, but she hadn't heard from Domenico—no apology, no link to the review, no confession of love…

But now he was standing outside.

Her first instincts were to hide. Hope he hadn't seen her inside. She was a mess after all day in the hot kitchen. She probably smelled, and she was far too conflicted right now to deal with whatever reason he was there.

But he was there. And every fiber in her being needed to know why.

She took a deep breath, squared her shoulders, then went to the door and opened it. "We're closed," she said, her voice tight.

"I'm in love with you."

He what?

Adriana's mouth dropped as she stared at Domenico for a long time.

Domenico shifted uncomfortably in the silence that continued to linger. He cleared his throat. "Can I—uh—come in?"

Right, he was still standing outside, and she'd essentially left him on read after his confession of love.

Adriana stepped back to let him enter. When the door closed behind him, she took a deep breath. "What are you doing here, Domenico?"

"I just told you. I'm here because despite my best efforts, I'm in love with you."

Despite his…

"That's romantic." Adriana folded her arms across her chest. After not believing her and accusing her of almost poisoning a guest, going silent for days, then showing up out of the blue with a confession of love, he was going to have to do a lot better than that. The whole Mr. Darcy thing might have worked in Jane Austen's era, but they'd already discussed this. Domenico could not pull that off.

"No, it isn't. Nothing about us is. But you had romance with Leo. You don't want romance," Domenico said, his usual challenge back in his tone.

The slight arrogance that used to annoy her was attractive right now. When had that shift occurred? How had Domenico Kasa's overblown ego gone from the thing that grated on her last nerve to the thing that made her want to fling herself into his arms and make out with him right now?

Maybe because she knew the man and the intentions and the vulnerability beneath it. She knew the heart of the boy she'd always loved beneath it.

Also, because he was right. Romance was for first loves—the ones meant to open one's heart, the ones meant to teach the lessons on how to love and be loved. It was to make the heartache worthwhile. At this stage in her life, she wanted truth and trust and a deep connection that surpassed romance to the level of *being* love for one another, embodying love.

She didn't want romance. She wanted the raw, passionate intensity they'd had that week on the island. Desperately craved it.

Still, he had work to do. And because heated tension defined their entire relationship, she rose to the challenge. "Then what do I want, Domenico?"

"You want a spark." He lowered his gaze and shook his head. "Screw that. You want a blazing flame. Like the one we have burning between us."

Adriana swallowed hard as she stared at him. She did want that. So much.

Domenico moved closer to her. He picked up a strand of her hair and twirled it around his finger, fighting for the right words. He took a deep breath, opened his mouth, shut it, then sighed.

When he finally spoke, the words came out gruff and sincere. "You drive me absolutely crazy. That sharp tongue of yours and your inability to ever be wrong… You are so stubborn all the damn time."

Really. Wow. "I'm stubborn? What about you? I've been gone almost a week, and you haven't reached out."

"I've wanted to. I've been going crazy without you."

Oh.

"I might have missed you a little bit," she said, the thick emotion in her voice calling her out.

Domenico caressed her cheek gently. "You were right, you know. You didn't make a mistake. Mrs. Conway added powdered shrimp to her husband's pasta."

Adriana's arms fell to her sides. Her expression was one of disbelief. "She tried to kill her husband?"

"We can't prove that, but based on the amount of effort she put into trying to sleep with me, I wouldn't be surprised. And likely she knew how quickly medics could arrive with the EpiPen. I think it was more a jealous rage thing to try to sabotage the resort review."

"Seems extreme. Rich people are crazy."

Domenico grinned. "Not all rich people. Anyway, the point is, I should have believed you."

"Is that an apology? Cause Leo sent six dozen roses…"

Domenico cut off her words, swooping in and pulling her into his arms. He stared into her eyes and brushed her hair away from her face.

Forget flowers.

Her heart raced and her pulse pounded as he held her close to his body and stared down into her eyes. The look of love and sincerity radiating in his expression nearly stole her breath.

"I'm sorry, Adriana. I'm sorry I treated you badly when you were with Leo. Seeing you with my brother killed me. You should have been with me instead. And then your complete disdain for me..."

"Can you blame me?" she whispered.

"No. And I'm sorry I didn't believe you were capable of running the kitchen. You are the perfect chef to run Kasa de Paradise's kitchen."

Adriana stiffened slightly. Was that why he was really there? To convince her to come work on the island permanently? Her stomach flipped...but surprisingly not entirely in a bad way.

Domenico touched her chin. "Not that I'm asking. I know you love your life here. This restaurant is your home. But if you won't consider the position on the island, at least give us a chance. You and me. I'll come back and forth. Maybe you can visit the island every other week—let Alex take the lead here in your absence? What do you say?"

It was nice in theory, but, "You never leave the island."

"I'm here now."

Adriana hesitated for a long moment, emotions evident on her face as she stared up at the man she was desperately falling in love with. "The chef position is still available?"

Domenico's expression lit up with cautious optimism. "For real? You'll come to Kasa de Paradise?"

Adriana surveyed her family restaurant from the corner of her eye. "Alex is right. Bellarini's needs to move into the next generation… He can do that better than I can."

Domenico nodded slowly. "So, you're taking the position because you're giving Alex the restaurant?"

Adriana wrapped her arms around Domenico's neck and rested her forehead against his chest. "I could take another position at a different restaurant if that was the reason."

"Then why?" he asked, his voice gruff and full of intensity.

Adriana kept her head pressed against his chest, unable to look up at him for fear that he'd see just how much she loved him written all over her face. "You really need me to say it?"

"I really do." Domenico placed a finger gently under her chin and lifted her face to look up at him. His gaze burned into hers with all the intensity and passion straight from his soul.

"Because I'm in love with you, Domenico."

Domenico smiled as he lowered his lips to hers. "About time you admitted it."

Adriana opened her mouth to say something, but Domenico silenced her with a kiss. Adriana sank into him and quit fighting the inevitable, returning his kiss with all the desire and love in her heart.

Giving in to the fact that she'd fallen for a paradise billionaire.

The right one this time.

* * * * *